THE
MEDUSA
PROTOCOL

ALSO BY ROB HART

Assassins Anonymous

The Paradox Hotel

The Warehouse

Take-Out: And Other Tales of Culinary Crime

Dark Space (with Alex Segura)

THE ASH MCKENNA SERIES

Potter's Field (Book 5)

The Woman from Prague (Book 4)

South Village (Book 3)

City of Rose (Book 2)

New Yorked (Book 1)

THE MEDUSA PROTOCOL

ROB HART

An Assassins
Anonymous Novel

G. P. PUTNAM'S SONS
NEW YORK

PUTNAM
—EST. 1838—

G. P. PUTNAM'S SONS
Publishers Since 1838
An imprint of Penguin Random House LLC
1745 Broadway, New York, NY 10019
penguinrandomhouse.com

Book design by Katy Riegel

Library of Congress Cataloging-in-Publication Data

Names: Hart, Rob, author.
Title: The Medusa protocol / Rob Hart.
Description: New York : G. P. Putnam's Sons, 2025. |
Series: An Assassins Anonymous Novel
Identifiers: LCCN 2024041743 (print) | LCCN 2024041744 (ebook) |
ISBN 9780593717424 (hardcover) | ISBN 9780593717431 (epub)
Subjects: LCGFT: Novels. | Thrillers (Fiction).
Classification: LCC PS3608.A7868 M44 2025 (print) |
LCC PS3608.A7868 (ebook) | DDC 813/.6—dc23/eng/20240909
LC record available at https://lccn.loc.gov/2024041743
LC ebook record available at https://lccn.loc.gov/2024041744

Printed in the United States of America
1   3   5   7   9   10   8   6   4   2

The authorized representative in the EU for product safety and
compliance is Penguin Random House Ireland, Morrison Chambers, 32
Nassau Street, Dublin D02 YH68, Ireland, https://eu-contact.penguin.ie.

To Todd

I learned it by watching you

We should be able to hold our suffering and look deeply into it, hold it tenderly and learn from it.

—THICH NHAT HANH

THE
MEDUSA
PROTOCOL

SOMEWHERE . . .

The shroud is ripped free, bright lights raking my eyes. I've been breathing through that fabric for at least a day, and it was developing an unpleasant funk. Before I can appreciate the fresh air, I'm shoved from behind.

With my hands bound behind my back, I can barely twist enough to stop from breaking my face on the floor. I manage to take the brunt of the fall on my shoulder, tucking my chin up and to the side to protect my head.

A rough pair of hands grab mine, and a cold blade slips between the delicate skin on the inside of my wrists, before slicing up and cutting the zip-tie. I twist around and crab-walk backward to create distance, thinking this might be followed by some kind of attack.

Instead, my captor is standing in the doorway, still as a monolith. He's a bundle of muscle so big it's almost grotesque, wearing black tactical gear and a white, featureless mask with dark lenses over the eyes. He looks like an owl with a steroid habit.

"Who are you?" I ask.

He tilts his head slightly to the side, like he doesn't understand what I'm saying. Which makes me think he doesn't speak English.

Not that I'm going to give up that easy.

"Why am I here?" I ask. "What do you want?"

He steps back and heaves a heavy steel door closed. There's a loud *shunk* as a locking mechanism engages.

And then I'm alone.

I climb to my feet, rubbing my wrists to get blood moving back into my hands, and survey the room. It's a cell. There's a stainless-steel toilet-sink combo in one corner. In the other, a metal cot juts from the wall, with a small foam mattress and a folded, threadbare blanket.

No windows, not even in the door. No shower. Perched on the sink is a travel-sized tube of toothpaste, so cheap it doesn't have a label, and a plastic cap covered in bristles that I can put over my finger; a prison toothbrush that can't be ground into a shank. There's a hotel-sized bar of soap, but no toilet paper.

I'm still in the same jeans and sweater and sneakers I was wearing when I was taken. Walking down Suffolk Street, to the Tuesday night meeting. My guard was down—I knew there was someone behind me, but it's New York, there's always someone behind you. Serves me right for thinking you can leave the life behind. I didn't clock the danger until I heard the scrape of a shoe on pavement, someone setting their weight to launch their body at me. I had barely registered the arms wrapping around my torso when a gleaming black van skidded to a halt at the curb.

I was thrown inside and the door slammed. The hood came down and my hands were quickly and efficiently zipped behind my back. A guttural voice got close to my ear and said, "Go along to get along."

Since then, not a word.

How long it's been, I don't know. Based on what I could hear—shuffling, clearing of throats—there were two people in the back of the van with me, and one person up front at the wheel. We drove for more than an hour. In traffic, then on a highway. We stopped and waited, the sound of the running engine lulling me into a state of calm, until something sharp pierced the skin of my neck. Then I disappeared into a twilight space, though not so far that I missed the unmistakable push of gravity shifting things around in my stomach.

We were airborne. At some point we landed, and then we drove some more. There was a noise so loud it made my skin vibrate, followed by a blast of wind whipping my clothes and then another shift in gravity. A helicopter.

The cobwebs in my head were finally clearing as the man in the mask marched me through this place, but my brain was still coming back online, sputtering in stops and starts. I couldn't tell much about the ambient climate, couldn't smell anything through the sodden mask, couldn't even think straight enough to count my steps.

Now that I've got my senses back, I can take better stock of my surroundings.

Something about the cell says "new construction." It smells like Sheetrock and fresh paint. The toilet and the reflective plate bolted in the wall above it, meant to be used as a mirror, are pristine and scratch-free. Everything is metal. The floors, the walls, the ceiling. There are curious seams in the floor, circles about three inches in diameter, at random intervals, and long horizontal slats on the walls, like venetian blinds.

Since this wasn't any kind of proper arrest, and the guard may not speak English, this most likely is a black site prison. The kind that operates outside laws and jurisdictions. No phone call, no lawyer. I know about a handful of places like this, but there are plenty I don't know about. If this one is new, trying to guess where I am isn't even worth the effort.

So I sit on the cot, exhausted, because being drugged and sleeping aren't the same thing. I do have to pee and consider using the toilet. I scan the cell one more time and find a small glass dome nestled in the corner of the ceiling, a tiny red light flashing behind the lens.

I wave at the camera. "Don't suppose you're going to tell me why I'm here?"

As if in response, there's a soft mechanical whir, and the slats on the wall slowly raise. Behind them is a massive white screen taking up three walls, which flickers to life and plays an array of swirls and patterns and colors that induce immediate feelings of dizziness and nausea.

So I look down at the floor, and those circular seams rise up—small pillars, no more than a few inches high each, making it impossible to walk freely. The cot tilts a few inches down and I nearly slip off, ensuring there'll be no way to sleep on it comfortably.

Before I can fully appreciate the level of thought that went into the discomfort of this place, a Celtic fiddle blares from hidden speakers, followed by a jaunty drumbeat.

Oh god.

"Come on Eileen" by Dexys Midnight Runners cuts through the room, bouncing off the hard surfaces, notes pelting me from every direction.

I take in my surroundings—the floor and the cot and the light show and the song and the camera through which someone is about to watch me pee—and I can't help but laugh.

Maybe it's the dying gasp of the drugs in my system. Maybe it's the realization that, after the type of life I lived, this is what I deserve. Just because you've decided to stop sinning doesn't mean you didn't sin.

And I have a very long list of sins.

I hope to meet the person who came up with this. I can't decide if I want to shake their hand or slit their throat. It's so diabolical as to deserve some kind of recognition.

The throat-slitting will depend on how many times I have to listen to this song, probably.

Even if that's a thing I'm not supposed to do anymore.

Even if sometimes I still want to do it.

In my time on this earth I have taken a lot of lives. One day I woke up and decided I didn't want to do that anymore. Every day I've woken up since then has felt like I was making that decision for the very first time.

That's the thing about being free from addiction. You're never free.

If there's one thing I wish I could do in this moment, it's convey to whoever my captors are how little this setup means to me. They get an A for effort, sure. I've seen torture, been tortured—this is some top-notch work and I expect it's not going to stop anytime soon.

But I have endured far, far worse than this.

And more than that, I endured those things alone.

This is me in my element.

I know what Mark would say right now. He would say: *You have tools, use them, figure out the next right action, and go from there.* Then we'd order takeout and put on a movie.

But Mark isn't here.

I

How can one expect a state of abundance to be everlasting?

—I CHING

MARK

Chinatown
One Month Later

We take our places around the statue of Dr. Sun Yat-sen in Columbus Park, everyone spreading out so we have room to move. As usual, I am the only white face, and the only person who doesn't qualify for an AARP card.

"Your form has been improving, but you're too much in your own head," Ms. Nguyen says, stretching her arms in the spot next to me. "Drop into it this time. Let everything else go."

"Just doing my best to keep up with you, sweetheart," I tell her.

Ms. Nguyen is wearing athletic pants and an oversize T-shirt, her gray hair tied back in a ponytail. Despite being in her seventies, the outfit makes her look like a kid. I'm in running shorts and a tank, the least modest outfit here. I tend to run hot, and by the time the class ends, the sun will have peaked the line of buildings and roared into the park.

"Remember," she says, "if you get overheated, you're welcome to take your shirt off."

"You're not worried about the other ladies getting jealous?"

She leans over and smacks the exposed flesh of my thigh. "I bring you here to show you off," she says.

Master Feng takes his place at the front of the group. He stands for a moment, in his cream-colored cotton uniform, his hands clasped behind his back. The man must be pushing ninety, but his eyes exude a penetrating sense of inner calm and presence, like he could count the droplets in a rainstorm.

He offers us a slight bow, and we all bow deeper as a sign of respect. Then he leads us through the opening movements, placing his arms out in front of him, before bringing them around to the right and toward his hip as he steps, delicately and deliberately, forward.

When Ms. Nguyen first suggested I do tai chi with her, I brushed it off. I know a dozen fighting styles, all of them designed to injure and kill as quickly and efficiently as possible. Tai chi looked to me like a bunch of old folks waving their arms around in a park.

And it's exactly that.

But it's more, too.

I've come to appreciate the gentleness of it. The focus of being in my body. Thinking of it less as a tool designed to inflict pain—which is something I spend every day actively working to forget—and seeing it more for what it is.

A tool in service of myself.

My own little temple, in which I can find peace.

I don't know the name for the movements we do, but I

watch Master Feng, and the men and women around me, as I try to emulate them and get lost in the flow.

The ache in my shoulder whistles in my ear, reminding me of the chunk of deltoid muscle that got torn out by a bullet. The practice has brought back some range of motion, more than physical therapy did. I'm able to move into the pain and then through it—like I'm manipulating something inside me, a little ball of energy I can toss from side to side.

Observing it and experiencing it without fighting it.

The getting out of my head part, that I'm still struggling with.

I called Astrid this morning, like I have every morning since she disappeared. I used to leave voicemails, then I stopped doing that. Today the robotic voice on the other end told me the line had been disconnected.

It was only a matter of time, I suppose.

It sounded like a period on the end of a sentence.

Confirmation she was back in the game, or dead.

For people like us, for me and Ms. Nguyen and the other members of our homegroup, I'm not sure if there are any other options. There's a reason working as a high-level assassin doesn't come with a 401(k) match.

Eventually, you cash out.

As we flow through a downward movement, Ms. Nguyen clears her throat. I glance over and she's tossing me a sharp eyebrow.

She doesn't need to say it. She can hear the gears grinding in my head.

Okay. Stay in the movement.

I follow Master Feng, try to match his energy, and let the surroundings fall away. For a little bit, it works. The ambulance screaming around the corner turns to a dull buzz. The kids playing in the adjoining park muffle into raindrops on a window.

I breathe deep and follow the peace of that breath.

Breathe in for four, hold for four, exhale for four, empty lungs for four.

Then I think about Astrid and it all goes to shit.

There's really not much to do at this point. I sit within the acceptance of it and continue the movements, enjoying the feel of my body brushing the dust off my muscles.

Another half hour, and we're done.

Master Feng bows to us, and we bow in return. The practitioners break into cliques, most of them rounding up expeditions for tea or dumplings.

A hand appears on my shoulder and I turn to find Master Feng. He offers me a serene smile. "Next time, less effort."

I bow to him again. "Thank you."

I'm not even sure if he heard it—he's off mingling with the other students, offering them words of affirmation. Ms. Nguyen appears in front of me, a sheen of sweat on her brow, but before she can say anything, an older woman grasps her arm, leans in to her ear, and says, "Tā hěn shuài."

He's handsome.

"Tā shì wǒ de," Ms. Nguyen responds.

He's all mine.

The woman scrunches up her face, looks at us both like she's discovered a conspiracy, and leaves.

"You know," I tell Ms. Nguyen, "I never said we were exclusive."

"I'm protecting you," she says. "That one would eat you for lunch."

"My hero." I offer her my arm. "May I escort you home, darling?"

She loops her arm into mine. "Of course."

The sun is out full blast now, June coming in hard. We wend our way through the streets of Manhattan, toward the West Village, navigating the morning crowds of commuters and tourists.

"I'm assuming Astrid didn't pick up the phone this morning," she says.

"Disconnected."

Ms. Nguyen gives a little shake of her head. "People go out."

"She was my sponsee. Which means she was my responsibility."

"The only person responsible for Astrid is Astrid. You can't take that on."

We stop at Canal Street, waiting for the light to change, letting the conversation drop as people crowd around us, knowing better than to say something that could be overheard by the wrong person.

Once we've crossed and we're clear of prying ears she says, "The point of sponsoring someone isn't to save them. It's to save yourself."

I respond by being obstinate and not saying anything.

Two blocks later she asks, "How's the new apartment?"

"It's fine. I like the East Village a little better than the West. It's quieter. Fewer drunken college kids."

"You sure it's safe to be here?" She nods up toward the glasses on my face. "Those things really work?"

I tilt them down at her. They look so stupid. Which is sort of the point. Thick black frames, wide lenses, the shape of them designed to screw with facial recognition software, by making it hard to take accurate measurements of my features. As an added layer, they project a low level of infrared light onto my face, so on CCTV, I'll appear slightly washed out and less identifiable.

"Been fully back three months and no one's killed me yet," I tell her. "Had a friend set up a new identity to overshadow my lack of an old one. But look, I live in acceptance of the fact that this is a risk. I was bored living up in the mountains. P. Kitty's not a good conversationalist."

"I'm glad you're back," she says. "I missed that cat."

"And you missed shamelessly hitting on me."

Ms. Nguyen smiles. "Sooner or later, you'll come around. Older women know what they want."

We make it to her building—my old building, too, before my apartment was firebombed in an attempt to draw me out of recovery—and she stops. She looks up at me and smiles. It's the way you would smile at a child who has just discovered some harsh reality about the world, like Santa isn't real.

"It's not your fault," she says.

"Feels like it is."

"Then you should talk about it tonight. See you later?"

"Wouldn't miss it."

She winks at me and heads inside. I watch her go, a little wistful for the life I had here. I really did love this building.

But, you know, the serenity to accept the things we cannot change, and all that.

My footsteps echo through the basement of St. Dymphna's, bouncing off the black-and-white checkerboard floor and the robin's-egg blue walls. I love the ritual of showing up early and setting up the space. Putting out the donuts, making the coffee. Dragging out the folding chairs and setting them in a circle.

One for Booker, our former Marine turned black ops mercenary. It's been more than five years since he's taken a life.

One for Valencia, formerly of the Special Operations Group, the covert paramilitary arm of the CIA. Seven years sober.

One for Ms. Nguyen, former employee of the Agency—a clandestine group of government agencies, and financial and industrial leaders. Retired ten years, sober sixteen.

One for Astrid, a former Agency hitter who operated under the name Azrael. She would have six months, and I put her chair out every week in case she shows up.

One for me. Formerly known as the Pale Horse, who, if you had asked my old bosses at the Agency, or anyone in the game really, was one of the best assassins in the world. Something that used to be a point of pride, and now is just an uncomfortable truth.

Finally, one for Kenji. Former Yakuza hitter, former chair of this group. My sponsor. Dead now, sacrificing both his recovery and his life to save mine a year and a half ago.

My friend.

I miss him so much.

Especially on days like today.

It does comfort me, putting his chair out, feeling his confident, gentle presence.

The same way Astrid's empty seat screws with my sense of inner peace.

The lights flicker, and Booker and Valencia enter, the two of them dressed for the summer heat: Valencia in yoga pants and a loose-fitting T-shirt, Booker in a black tank and camo pants. Valencia is pushing the baby stroller that Booker and I got for her baby shower. It cost what most people would spend on a month's rent, but that little girl in there only gets the best.

Valencia had wanted to be a mom for a long time. It's why she stopped killing, why she got into recovery. She didn't want to be a mom who killed people. And every week she would unpack that.

One day she decided she was ready, she found a donor, and: Lucia.

Born three short weeks ago.

That baby isn't just a milestone for Valencia. She is a tiny, breathing, sometimes-screaming example that the program works. She bound us tighter, giving us someone to love together. It's personal, too; I can't ever see my son, and every day that feeling twists like a blade in my stomach. I will do whatever it takes to make sure this kid grows up safe and loved.

Valencia rolls the stroller up to me. Lucia is swaddled in a blanket, snoozing away. The wisps of black hair on her head are thickening. "She's looking more like you and less like a potato," I tell her.

Valencia beams when I say this.

I like her smile. She didn't used to smile this much.

Booker slaps me on the back, a little too hard, but exactly as hard as I would expect him to. "How are we today, Uncle Mark?"

"Good, Uncle Booker. How about you?"

"I never signed off on her calling either of you 'uncle,'" Valencia says, adopting her usual look of barely restrained contempt.

"That's why I'm going to keep on saying it," Booker says. "She'll pick it up through osmosis."

The lights flicker again, and Ms. Nguyen comes in, carrying a plate of shortbread cookies, which she places next to the donuts. I've given up on telling her not to do that; no one eats the donuts, then I have to take them home, and I spend the whole week trying to finish them before I have to buy more. It's too many carbs.

I could always stop buying them, but, habits.

That's why we're here. It takes work to break them.

Sometimes the best way to do that is to replace them with other habits.

Valencia and Ms. Nguyen step away to get themselves settled and coo over the baby. Booker glances over at the chairs and asks, "Anything?"

I shake my head. "Number was disconnected."

"Shit." He sighs, his shoulders sagging. "Might be time to put away her chair."

"Not until I know, one way or the other."

"I know what you're doing," Booker says. "Kenji lost sponsees, too. Difference was, he didn't blame himself."

"I'm not blaming myself."

"You're a shitty liar."

"Out of practice, I guess."

Booker surveys our little group. "Maybe it wasn't for her. Six months, she never shared."

"You don't have to share to be here."

"But did she *want* to be here?"

When I can't come up with a good answer, Booker pats me on the chest and points a nonthreatening finger in my face. "Share about it, okay? The only way out is through."

"The through part sucks," I tell him.

We make our way to the circle of chairs and sit. I take out the lipstick-sized transmitter from my pocket, switch it on, and place it on the floor next to me. It'll serve to prevent any other devices from listening or recording the things we say.

And then I start:

"Assassins Anonymous is a fellowship of men and women who share their experience, strength, and hope with each other, that they may solve their common problem and help each other to recover. The only requirement for membership is a desire to stop. We are not allied with any sect, denomination, politics, organization, or institution; our primary purpose is to stop killing and help others to achieve the same.

"We do not bring weapons into Assassins Anonymous, nor prior political affiliations. If any of us were known by any particular handle or nickname, we do not use it here. We share our stories, but we obscure details as best we can. If any of us seek to bring in new fellows, we agree to have them properly vetted. This is to protect us, not just from prying ears, but from each other."

We take a moment of silence for fallen comrades.

No one ever suggested we should. We just know to do it.

"Valencia," I ask, "could you read the steps?"

Valencia shifts in her seat and closes her eyes. In a normal AA meeting, you'd read from a handout, but we like to avoid putting things in writing.

"We really gotta do this every time?" Booker asks.

"You really got to ask that every time, B? Remember what Kenji said: 'We have steps to keep us from killing ourselves, and traditions to keep us from killing each other.' Valencia?"

Booker smiles. He's being difficult, but he knows it, too.

Traditions.

Valencia begins:

"One, we admitted we were powerless—that our lives had become unmanageable.

"Two, we came to believe that a power greater than ourselves could restore us to sanity.

"Three, we made a decision to turn our will over to the care of a higher power, as we understood it.

"Four, we made a searching and fearless moral inventory of ourselves.

"Five, we admitted to our higher power, to ourselves, and to another human being the exact nature of our wrongs.

"Six, we were ready to have our higher power remove all these defects of character.

"Seven, we humbly asked it to remove our shortcomings.

"Eight, we made a list of all persons we had harmed, and became willing to make amends to them all.

"Nine, we made direct amends to such people wherever possible, except when to do so would injure them or others.

"Ten, we continued to take personal inventory, and when we were wrong promptly admitted it.

"Eleven, we sought through prayer and meditation to improve our conscious contact with our higher power as we understood it, praying only for knowledge of its will for us and the power to carry that out.

"Twelve, having had a spiritual awakening as the result of these steps, we tried to carry this message to others like us, and to practice these principles in all our affairs.

"No one among us has been able to maintain anything like perfect adherence to these principles. We are not saints . . ."

Booker and I chuckle, because, traditions.

"The point is that we are willing to grow along spiritual lines," Valencia says.

When she's done she puts her hand on the stroller, but Lucia hasn't stirred.

"Okay," I say, "so before we get started, any announcements or topics we need to discuss?" When no one says anything, I ask, "Who would like to share first?"

Booker crosses his arms.

Valencia raises an eyebrow.

Ms. Nguyen smirks.

All of those actions, heat-seeking missiles directed straight at me.

Fine.

"I'm Mark, and I haven't killed anyone in two and a half years," I say.

"Hi, Mark," Booker says in a slightly mocking tone, his voice ringing through the space.

"You're such a dipshit," I tell him, and he laughs. "Valencia, I think you're the only one I didn't tell this to, but Astrid's phone is disconnected. I'm really struggling with that today. These programs, obviously, are pretty small, so I feel like the act of taking on a sponsee . . . it's pretty intimate. You feel like your recovery is connected to theirs. And I know what all the literature says, I know what you're all saying, that it's not my fault, but it's easy to say and not so easy to believe. I just wish I could talk to her. See where she's at. I've even gone onto the Amber Road . . ."

"Mark," Booker says, clearly upset I'm back on the website— a darknet marketplace for anything from weapons to drugs to kill contracts. Something all of us are supposed to avoid.

"Crosstalk," Valencia says, scolding Booker for interrupting my share.

"Thanks, V. I know I'm not supposed to be on there. I know it's like walking into a bar and telling myself I'm just going to have a cranberry juice. I'm fine with the cranberry juice. I don't feel tempted to work. I just want to find some kind of sign, and it's the only way I can think to do it. See if Azrael has popped back up. But, nothing. She just disappearing into thin . . ."

The lights flicker again, and my pulse immediately amps up.

A year and a half ago, I was attacked after a meeting. Part

of a plot to draw me out and get me back into the killing life. It's why Kenji is dead and my shoulder is jacked, but it also brought me and Astrid together, and got her into the program.

Shortly after I took over as chair of the weekly meetings, the archdiocese decided this broken-down church wasn't worth maintaining anymore. So I bought it. It felt like a good thing to do with all that blood-drenched money sitting in my safe.

We could have found a new home for our meetings, but I didn't want to. Because this is where these people saved me after I accidentally killed an innocent man, and nearly took my own life as a form of atonement.

In the process of buying this place I made some upgrades to ensure our safety. If we were exposed once, it could happen again. The flickering light is a gentle notification that someone is coming in through the front door. All of us know this, but we also know that no one else is due to be joining the meeting.

Whoever it is, they're walking into a room of trained killers.

Reformed, sure, but still not a smart move.

Footsteps echo from the doorway and I pray to see Astrid.

Instead it's a tall Hispanic kid with a shaved head, barely out of his teens, wearing basketball shorts and a tank top. He pokes his head in and surveys the lot of us, then steps into the room, hoisting a pizza box.

"Mark?" he asks.

"Yeah," I say, getting up, my senses kicked into overdrive.

He tentatively steps forward, holding the box aloft. "Delivery."

His arms aren't straining against the weight of it, so I doubt it's some kind of explosive device. He looks confused but not scared. Just like anyone would be confused, delivering a pizza to the basement of a church.

"From who?" I ask.

"Whom," Ms. Nguyen mutters.

The kid shrugs. "I just deliver them, man."

I take the box from him and give it a little jostle. It's warm and humid. I bring it to the table with the donuts, set it down, and open it up to find a large pie, covered in olives.

Only monsters put olives on pizza.

And Astrid.

"Where did you get this?" I ask.

"The pizza place I work for?" the kid says, clearly befuddled. "It's just a delivery."

"Who called it in?"

"I don't answer the phones, man. I got, like, three more to do so . . ."

Booker is at my side now, looking down at the pie. He looks back and forth between us and I tell him, "That's Astrid's order."

He nods. "She's alive."

A soft buzzing alarm rings from the cabinet in the corner of the room, and my racing heart slams to a near stop.

The lights mean someone is at the front door.

The buzz means someone is coming in from the roof.

I dash to the metal cabinet in the corner, insert the key, unlock it, and throw the doors open. The video feeds are lit up; there are three black SUVs outside, idling at the curb. Upstairs, in the office space formerly used by the priests, there are eight men in tactical gear; they must have climbed down from the apartment next door and gotten in through a window, tripping the alarm in the process.

Three of them are carrying Benelli M4s. The Rolls-Royce of combat shotguns, and they'll punch a basketball-sized hole through anyone not wearing a vest. The rest are carrying LMT CSWs—nasty compact rifles with subsonic .300 Blackout chambering and shrouded suppressors.

None of that gear is cheap.

They're professionals.

Booker appears next to me. "How many?"

"Eight upstairs," I tell him. "Can't tell how many out front."

No one needs to be told.

We all get it.

Looking, in unison, at Lucia, sleeping in her stroller.

Before I can even ask him to, Booker is across the room, opening a hatch in the floor. The lid falls back with a *clang*, which makes the delivery kid jump, and it wakes up Lucia, who starts wailing.

The SUVs are still waiting at the curb, same as the men upstairs. They must have someone looking for a way to kill the lights. It won't take them long to figure it out.

I grab a Glock 43 from the cabinet and hand it to Ms. Nguyen.

"Just in case," I tell her, and she checks to make sure it's loaded.

Valencia is already strapping Lucia to a harness hanging from her chest, as the pizza delivery kid is staring at the screens, hands on his head, muttering a string of curses.

I pat him on the back. "Hey, what's your name?"

"Julio," he says, without looking at me.

"Okay, Julio. Not much time to explain. You're going to go down that hatch with Valencia and Ms. Nguyen. There's a subbasement, which leads into an old Prohibition tunnel, which will bring you to the basement of an apartment building a few blocks away."

He looks around the room, too confused and panicked to focus on anything. "I don't know . . . I don't know . . ."

"Julio." I give him a soft smack on the cheek, and that makes him look at me. His eyes are so wide it's a marvel they're still in his head. "You drew the short straw tonight, bud. I'm sorry. Those people outside will kill you without hesitation. We're not going to let that happen, but you have to listen to everything we say. Do you understand?"

He nods and runs for the hatch, stumbling as he seeks purchase on the ladder.

Valencia stands at the mouth of the tunnel. "You and Booker can come, too."

"We're going to hold them off."

Lucia is still screaming, her face wrinkled and red. Valencia puts a hand on her head, to try and calm her. "Try not to kill any of them, okay?"

I touch the top of Lucia's head. She is so warm and so soft and so beautiful.

"We're going to do whatever we have to," I tell her. "Now go."

I can see it on Valencia's face; she wants to argue. She doesn't want to leave us behind.

But she understands the crushing gravity of this, so she

heads down the hatch after Julio. Ms. Nguyen is the last to go. As she's descending I tell her, "If they get past us, you give 'em hell, okay, sweetheart?"

She offers a sly little grin. "See you soon, Mark."

Once she's clear, I close the hatch. There's a lock, which I don't bother clasping; if they make it to the door it'll barely slow them down. I wish I'd gotten the chance to finish the last part of my plan, which was to line the shaft with explosives. That way, once everyone was clear, it could be blown and ensure no one would be able to follow.

When I thought of it, it seemed like a bit much.

Now I realize none of it was enough.

I run back to the cabinet and gear up: a night vision mask, a level-three ballistics vest, and a fully automatic paintball gun with a two-hundred-round hopper. Booker has a similar paintball gun, as well as a Mossberg 500 shotgun strapped to his back, packed with rubber slugs. I grab a collapsible baton, then get to work situating all the gear.

Once everything is secured, I turn to Booker. We linger, for a moment, in the recognition of what's about to happen.

The appreciation that we're in this together.

"Whatever it takes," he says.

He doesn't need to explain it.

When you get into the killing life, you do a moral inventory: what you'll kill for, who you'll die for.

You do the same when you enter the program. A part of you understands that one day you might have to sacrifice your recovery for someone.

Like Kenji did for me.

Like both of us will, right now, for Lucia.

She lives.

Even if we have to kill every single one of these mother-fuckers.

"Whatever it takes," I tell him.

The lights click off, plunging the basement into darkness.

"Okay," Booker says, with the resignation of someone looking at an unmowed lawn. "Let's work."

ASTRID

Albuquerque
Twenty-Two Years Ago

A beat-up Jeep Cherokee the color of an old forest cruises down the block, like the people inside are looking for an address. The windows are tinted so I can't see them, but I don't think they can see me, dressed head to toe in black, standing in a pool of shadow at the edge of the park.

It's just past two A.M. The dealers are winding down for the night, and the cops don't tend to come here unless necessary. People don't call this neighborhood "the War Zone" because it's nice.

The ranch-style house across the street seems to decay further the more I look at it, the rot creeping across in real time. The screens on the door are ripped, the windows that aren't broken are replaced by cardboard. Weeds grow wild out of the cracked pavement.

I run my hand across the pocket of my jeans, feeling the

bulge of the switchblade, then slip my hand inside to grasp the handle. A talisman, granting me courage.

Then I walk toward the house, keeping watch on the windows, the street, for any signs of light or movement.

A broken gate leads to the backyard, and I slip through without moving it, then creep low underneath the bedroom window, until I'm in a sea of tall brown grass and broken furniture. As I make my way toward the sliding glass door, something big shifts up from the ground, and I'm staring at a massive Rottweiler. It offers a low growl that starts threatening, then quickly grows confused.

"Rocky," I say, offering my hand, even though this might be a mistake. "You remember me, Rocky, don't you?"

The dog's eyes fix on me and it gives another little growl, and I think, okay, maybe this wasn't the best idea, but then the dog comes trotting over, its tongue lolling out of its mouth. It reaches the length of its chain, about ten feet away. I close the distance, kneel down, and accept a big, sloppy, wet tongue on my face.

"I missed you, too," I tell him, scratching him behind the ears.

I run my hand over his muscular back. He was so much smaller, the last time I saw him . . .

Push it away. I get up and move toward the glass door. There's a filthy gray curtain hanging on the inside. I give the handle a little nudge, and it doesn't move. There's a window a little farther down, slightly ajar. I creep over and peek inside the kitchen, then slide it up slowly, so it doesn't make a sound.

I snake through the window. It's easy for me. I've done

enough crawling and climbing for a lifetime, my body used to getting away from danger. For the first time I'm going toward it, and somehow it feels a little like the same thing.

I slide off the counter and onto the floor, nearly gagging on the thick smell of food decomposing in the trash, dirty dishes growing mold colonies in the sink. There are flies in the air. I listen for any sounds other than the buzzing, like someone might have been alerted to my presence.

Hearing none, I move toward the bedroom. On the kitchen counter is a cheap chef's knife with a white plastic handle, encrusted with days-old peanut butter. It's a little less sturdy than the switchblade, but I like the size of it, so I grab it off the counter and hold it against my forearm.

And as I tiptoe toward the bedroom I wait for it to hit: that feeling like I should run.

Like I shouldn't be doing this. That this is wrong.

I've never killed anyone before.

Shouldn't I be feeling some sense of trepidation? Second thoughts?

What does it say about me that I don't?

All I see is the clarity of the task before me, and then tomorrow, I will be healed. I will be done with this. I get to make a new life for myself.

I just have to do this one thing, and then I'm free.

The door is open. There's only one body in the bed, under a bunched white sheet.

Him.

That sandy mop of hair. That thick beard that always smelled like cigarettes and rum. I move around to the side of the bed and consider waking him. Consider asking him all the questions I've wondered almost every day for the last six years.

How much was I worth, in actual dollars and cents?

Did you ever miss me?

Why?

I don't care to hear the answers. Not from him, at least. So I raise the knife, ready to plunge it into the soft part of his throat. I hesitate, wondering, *Can I do this?*

And realize: *Of course I can.*

His eyes snap open.

They lock on mine and in that moment I'm a child again, terrified of the wrath that would come out of nowhere, like a summer storm. In a state of bleary confusion, he mutters, "Emma?"

His eyes dart from mine to the knife, now hovering in the air, and his eyes go wider. Realization dawns, and in a flash his hand comes out from under his pillow with a small black revolver.

I react a second too slow. By the time I shake off the fear and bring the knife down, my forearm slams into his, the point of the blade hovering a few inches from his face, the barrel of the gun pointed just shy of my head.

Even though I'm above him and I have the leverage, he's still twice my size. He pushes my arm back, hard enough the knife slips from my grasp and flies across the room, clattering into a corner. He glances to follow its trajectory, so I take that moment of distraction to climb on top of him, pinning down the gun, putting both my hands over it, and wresting it from his grip.

The gun fires, a massive sound in such a small space. The bullet slams into the headboard, the room suddenly filling with the acrid smell of gunpowder. The shock and sound rings through my body. That might draw attention, but then again, in this neighborhood, maybe not.

I keep the pressure on the gun, pressing it down into his hand and the mattress, so the barrel can't load a new round. Rocky barks outside, and there's another sound. Someone's screaming.

I'm screaming.

All that rage inside me bubbling up, finally finding the outlet it deserves.

But still, he's twice my size. He flips me around and throws me onto the bed, pinning me down, the gun lost now, and every cell in my body explodes at the memory of this, at the feeling of it, at what came next when I was pinned down to the bed and he was standing over me with that look in his eye, with rum on his breath. He reaches down, trying to find the gun, which is all the opening I need to pull the switchblade out of my jacket pocket and jam it into the side of his neck.

Everything stops, and the only thought in my head is: *That was easier than I thought.* Not the ending-his-life part, that I've been committed to for going on two years.

I just thought it would take more force to pierce his skin.

He stumbles off me, coughing, his hand on the knife, blood spitting between his lips, pouring between his fingers as they slip on the handle. He looks at me, like he wants to say something, and his eyes are flooded with fear.

Good.

That was the entire point of this.

For him to feel how I felt.

The blood is soaking his white T-shirt and boxers, and he falls back to the floor with a hard *thump,* coming to a rest against the dresser, and I don't know how long it takes but I watch the whole time, as the life leaves him and his body slumps to the ground, and behind me, there's a scream . . .

ASTRID

Brazil, Maybe?
Four Hours Before the Pizza Arrives

We went back too far."

That's all I can remember. Those words, floating on the air like smoke, somewhere above my head. A man said them. He had an accent, I think? It's hard to be sure.

I sit up slowly. I've learned to not sit up too quickly on the days that I wake up in this cell with fragments of sentences bouncing around my head. The first time I woke up and stood up too fast, I vomited, and they waited a day to clean it up.

At least, I think it was a day. Still don't know how long I've been in here. I don't know how much time passes when I'm unconscious. Don't know how long ago they stuck me in here. A month? Maybe more?

I'm only ever taken out of this room for two reasons. The protrusions will retract into the floor, the screens will flick off, and most mercifully of all, the song will stop playing. Then a guard will show up to take me for a shower—or there's a hissing sound, a smell like wildflowers, and then I'm unconscious for an indeterminate amount of time, until I wake up here.

And as soon as I'm settled, or I'm awake, the cycle starts again.

On cue, the patterns appear on the screens, and I drop my eyes to the floor, watching the protrusions slide into place. "Come on Eileen" blares from the walls. I sing along under my breath. That's made it a little more tolerable. Like I'm participating, rather than letting it happen.

I navigate a safe path to the sink, rinse my face in the meager stream, then try to drink some of it. On the lip of the sink is the single tine of the black plastic fork I broke off from my first meal here. I stoop down to the floor, where I carefully scratch a single line, next to the nine other lines.

So that's ten times now, that I was taken from this room for . . . something.

I've stopped checking my body for bruises or injuries. It's never the outside parts of me that hurts. It's in that most delicate space, behind my ribs and between my lungs.

Except, this time, I've got something.

"We went back too far."

That's helpful.

Fragmented memories, like jigsaw pieces dumped on the floor, sour on the tip of my tongue when I wake up, they're not just my brain distracting me. Someone is looking for something; rifling through the filing cabinet in my brain.

And whatever they want, they don't want me to *know* they want it—or else they wouldn't put me under. They don't want me to remember the questions. So it's sensitive information. I wish that helped narrow it down, but my line of work put me in countless need-to-know situations.

The song stops.

Then it starts again.

Now that I've got my wits a little more about me, I consider moving my body. There are ways to combat the effects of torture, and physical activity is one. There's not much I can do in the way of cardio, but calisthenics have kept me sane.

Dips off the cot. Handstand push-ups. Squats.

As I'm trying to decide what to do first, the bottom of the door opens, and a metal tray slides in. I pick it up and put it on my lap. A dozen dumplings and a small carton of water. I don't get any more plastic forks. They let me keep the little piece I broke, and they must see me using it on the camera, but I guess they figured I could have one toy.

The dumplings are good. They always are. It's the only thing they've given me to eat. I imagine because it's a decent mix of carb, protein, and fat. But my calorie intake is lower than it used to be. The waistband of my jeans is a little loose. There's just enough water, too—as much as it takes to keep me alive, and likely no more than that. I drink half the carton and save the rest for later.

I glance up at the camera, smile, and wave.

Nothing about the time I've spent here is fun, but it pales in comparison to a week in a survival, evasion, resistance, and escape school. SERE training was established in the aftermath of the Korean War, meant to keep soldiers sharp and resistant to torture. It's more an elaborate, cruel hazing ritual than it is actual training. But it still involved being hooded, beaten by unseen assailants, kept awake for days, starved until I could barely think, and then stripped naked and left soaking wet in the cold December air.

I got through that.

I got through worse than that.

I can get through this.

When I'm finished with my food I put the empty tray on the floor next to the door.

I get three meals a day and I get a shower every three days. *Days* being a relative term in a place where time has ceased to exist. This was meal number eight since my last shower. Which means in a few minutes a guard will show up.

It's always just me and the guard. No one else. No windows anywhere. I've spent hours with my ear to the door, and even over the constant droning of Dexys Midnight Runners, I've been able to pick up snippets of conversation. Guards speaking to each other in Portuguese. From the accent and the slang, I'm guessing somewhere in Brazil.

Other than that?

Nothing.

A great number of highly powerful people want to kill me. I haven't even gotten close to my eighth step, in which I create a list of all the people I've wronged, to whom I need to make amends. Not that it would help much. It's going to be a long list.

But whoever is doing this has to be connected. Someone working in tandem with a government entity, or someone who is very, very wealthy. Those are the only kinds of people who could afford to stick me into a state-of-the-art black site that is maybe in Brazil.

At this point, the *who* matters slightly less to me than the *why*.

Everything about this is uncomfortable, but despite stubbing my toes a few times on the floor, nothing about this is painful. If you want to hurt someone, fingernails are a good place to start. This feels both excessive and pointless.

"One day at a time," I mutter to myself.

Which makes me think about Mark and the others. I wonder if they're looking for me. I wonder if they've already given up on me. Figured I went out or was killed. They've probably moved on, and I wouldn't blame them . . .

There's a scraping sound from the door, and then a *click*.

The slats on the wall close and the song stops playing. The protrusions lower into the floor. The guard who opens the door, I've come to know. He's the one who put me in the room in the first place. Since then I've been able to take in some more details. Scarring on his hands, busted up from a lifetime of fighting. Black curls of hair peek around the mask. I've taken to calling him Godfrey, after the sadistic chain-gang boss in *Cool Hand Luke*.

Mark would be so proud of me. He does love a good movie reference.

But it also conveys on him some degree of humanity, which the mask was designed to take away.

I look up at him and ask, "Hey, Godfrey. Are you going to tell me why I'm here today?"

He stands silent as a stone, waiting for me to put my arms behind my back. I give it a beat, trying to hide my excitement.

At the mistake he made today.

"Guess not," I tell him.

He takes my hands—gently, as he always does—and cuffs me, then leads me into the hallway. As we make our way to the shower room, I do the same thing I always do: count my steps (sixty-seven) and the doors I pass (four). There's another door at the end of the curved hall, with a keypad. That must be the exit.

Without knowing the layout of this place, without having a better sense of the routines, without having access to any kind of tools or help, all I've been able to do is wait for the one thing that could save me: human error.

I caught one already; despite there being cameras in the cells, there aren't any in this hallway.

It hasn't been worth trying to overpower Godfrey. Even with my hands tied behind my back, I probably could. He looks tough, but that only ever means so much. The problem is, what would I do with what would assuredly be a temporary freedom?

How bad would they punish me for acting out?

If I'm going to make a move, it has to be worth it. I have to gain something in the process.

And today, it might be worth it.

Because when he walked into my cell, I noticed the rectangular-shaped bulge in his pocket.

He's carrying his cell phone.

He's never carried anything in his pockets before. Probably

a safety measure mandated by the prison, to prevent inmates from getting their hands on them. Maybe he forgot, or he was in a rush, but either way, my salvation lies in his pocket and I just have to find a way to get it from him.

We reach the shower room and he opens the door, allowing me to enter. It's a blank metal room, much like my cell, with a single showerhead built into the ceiling, above a drain. I don't get soap in here. I don't take off my clothes, either; I'm still wearing the same outfit in which I was taken, and I'm allowed to rinse off for five minutes, with my hands still cuffed. It seems like a mercy, not having to strip naked in front of a stranger. Though I'm less touchy about some random guard seeing my tits than I am the scar that snakes down my back. That feels far too intimate.

It's only a mercy until I'm returned to my cell, where the temperature will be turned down to just enough above freezing that I don't die, but drying out will be both long and uncomfortable.

What I would do for some soap, a little conditioner, a clean set of clothes. The showers don't do all that much at this point. I feel the grime in my skin, my clothing having gone brittle and stiff. My jeans are coated in dried blood—my request for pads or tampons last week fell on deaf or indifferent ears. I tried washing my clothes in the sink, but that used up all the soap, and I only get soap every twelfth meal, which means every four days. And soap is precious, since they don't give me toilet paper.

I step under the water and enjoy the burst of warmth, let it run down my hair and soak my clothes. Then I turn to Godfrey and ask, "So do you speak English?"

He pauses a little, like he's considering what I'm saying.

"This place sucks. I'm writing a shitty Yelp review when I get out of here."

As I talk, I work the cuffs behind me, twirling the chain on itself, letting the sound of the water and my voice cover up the clinking of the metal. Another trick I learned in SERE training: if you bind the chain tightly enough, you can apply leverage to make it snap. It works better on high-quality cuffs. Low-quality cuffs will bend while the hardened steel of higher quality is more prone to snapping.

These feel expensive.

I can do it with my eyes closed—when my hands are in front of me.

Behind me is a different story.

"So what do I have to do to get a meal other than dumplings?" I ask.

He shakes his head a little. Is there a smile under that mask? Maybe.

Probably about four minutes left? This isn't an exact science, and sometimes it takes a few minutes spinning the chains on the cuffs to get a proper bind. I won't know until I can't move my hands, and then I'll have to hope I can create enough leverage. Hope I don't hurt or dislocate something in the process.

I rack my brain for something to talk about.

What would Mark do? Mark is a talker. I'm not much of a talker.

"So," I ask, "você fala português?"

Do you speak Portuguese?

[43]

"Sim," he says quickly, without thinking.

Yes.

"Eu sabia," I tell him.

Knew it.

He shuffles a bit, looks down at the floor. He's made another mistake. He's not supposed to talk to me. He's not supposed to be carrying his cell phone, either, and he's going to realize it in a moment, if I can get these damn chains . . .

There.

My hands lock up, the chains bound on themselves.

"Por que estou aqui?" I ask.

Why am I here?

He tilts his head like he wants to speak, but he doesn't answer. I nod, then look past him, squinting at the far wall, hoping to draw his attention away from me.

"O que é aquilo?" I ask.

What is that?

It works. Lulled into a false sense of security, he turns to glance at nothing. I push my elbows forward and bear down hard on my hands, bringing them up and past my rear, like I'm trying to break a pair of zip-ties.

The cuffs snap, freeing my arms, and by the time he turns around, he sees me coming at him with my knee out. I throw it hard into his gut, and lucky for me, he's not wearing any kind of protective gear; probably doesn't need it down here in what I assume is solitary, so my kneecap imprints cleanly onto his spine.

He stumbles into the wall behind him, hitting it hard. I come down and slip on the accumulated water on the floor, and in the second it takes me to regain my footing, he's squared up. He pulls out the electrical baton hanging from his hip, holding it forward but not activating it.

There's too much water in here. He knows it's not safe.

Another thing I was counting on.

But he could still swing it hard enough to do some damage. Meanwhile, I'm underslept, in a calorie deficit, and, despite my workout routine, have been locked in a cell for a month.

This will be fun.

Godfrey is big and he's strong but he's slow. When he swings the baton at my head in a wide arc it's easy enough to slip underneath it and move to his left side, while simultaneously driving my fist into his liver. He arches into the pain, protecting his body, and tries to swing the baton again, so I drop myself toward the floor, landing on my side, then swing my legs hard behind his knees.

He goes airborne, landing hard on his back, sending up a splash of water.

I climb on top of him and rip off the mask before he can get his bearings. He's handsome, in a boyish way, with a wispy attempt at a beard. I pull him up toward me as I bring down my elbow, smashing him square in the face, breaking his nose in the process. Blood gushes from his nostrils as his eyes swirl around in their sockets.

I take a second to catch my breath, which is a mistake, because he bucks his hips, throwing me up and over him. I land in the middle of the shower stream, water filling my eyes and nose and mouth, and roll to the side—just in time to avoid his boot coming down where my head was.

I combat roll into a standing position, getting to my feet as he charges. Just before he hits me, I jump, manage to grab a pipe hanging from the ceiling. It's blazing hot and sears my palms, but I hold on and bring my foot up, connecting under his chin.

That one rings his bell.

He goes down in a heap. He's not fully unconscious, but he's not getting up anytime soon, either. I drop to the floor and kick away the baton, then roll him onto his stomach, root around in his pockets until I find the cell phone.

No service.

Of course. The walls are made of metal. This place is one big Faraday cage.

I take the baton. I don't want to use it. Electric weapons are dangerous—it's rare that they put people into cardiac arrest, but it can happen. Even if it's an accident, I'd still be making the choice to take the risk, and then it would be back to counting days.

Still, the threat of it should be enough.

I pull him to his feet and get behind him, put the stun stick against his neck.

"Você sente isso?" I ask.

Do you feel that?

He nods his head.

"A porta do corredor. Onde isso leva?" I ask.

The door in the hallway. Where does it lead?

"Escadaria," he says.

Stairs.

"Posso chegar ao telhado?"

Can I get to the roof?

"Sim."

"Okay. Vamos."

I keep the business end of the stick pressed into his neck. He leads me into the hall and takes me to the scanner. I don't need to ask. He keys in the code. It turns green and the door unlocks.

"Fique encostado na parede," I tell him. "Inversão de marcha. Qaul é o código do telefone."

Stand against the wall. Turn around. What's the code to the phone?

"Dois-dois-sete-nove."

I click in 2-2-7-9 and the phone opens. With that settled, and before he can get any bright ideas, I run through the door and slam it behind me.

At least he wasn't lying. Motion sensor lights flicker on, illuminating a stairwell. A mix of metal and concrete. I was right about the new construction; there's still Sheetrock dust in the corners. Still no signal, though. I head up, passing three floors, before getting to a ladder and a hatch. There's a key code on this one. I try the code Godfrey used downstairs—3-1-9-0—but the pad turns red and makes an angry buzzing noise.

I smack the side of the casing with my fist. Once, twice.

It doesn't budge.

I lower myself down a bit, take out the baton, and wail on it. The shock of it travels up my arm. This is possibly dumb—if the baton breaks and I get electrocuted—but a door opens somewhere at the bottom of a stairwell, and frenzied footsteps march up the stairs.

One more solid whack, and the casing breaks, falling about six inches, suspended in the air by the wires inside. I dig through them until I manage to short it out and undo the lock.

Then I turn the crank on the door. It takes the full weight of my body pushing up to get it open.

That first blast of fresh air, that warmth of the sunlight on my face are luxurious.

I climb out, blinking against the brightness. It takes my eyes a moment to adjust.

When they do, I don't like what they see.

I'm standing atop a large, circular, concrete building. There are two more nearby, connected by tunnels. In the middle there appears to be some kind of recreation yard, with a small circular track and some free weights scattered about.

There's no barbed wire. No high walls surrounding the compound. No real sense of any kind of prison security. It's the view around us that explains why: jungle, rocky shores, and empty ocean in every direction. The wind is whipping so hard off the water it's difficult to draw a full breath.

I open the phone and check the map icon, then search for my current location. It shows a pulsing blue dot off the coast of Brazil, not too far from São Paulo. So I got that much right. According to the date I've been in that room for a month.

One thing breaks in my favor.

It's a Tuesday.

Tuesday means AA. It's four P.M. here, which means it's three P.M. in New York. Four hours until the meeting. I consider calling Mark or Booker—I don't have Valencia's or Ms. Nguyen's numbers memorized—but once I'm found out, and it won't be long, they'll be able to pull up the call history, even if I delete it.

If I could get them a message . . .

That could put them in danger. But there's no one else I can contact. I'm on the outs with the Agency. For all I know they put me here.

I'm alone.

You're not alone, Mark would say.

Okay. It has to be something they'll understand but will be harder on this end to figure out. And then I remember how goddamn obnoxious Mark can be about pizza.

I dial the pizza place around the corner from the church. An older man with a gruff voice answers: "Authentic Ray's."

"Hey . . . hey," I say, my heart just cracking open at the sound of something familiar. "I need to order a pizza for to-night. Large, extra olives."

"Address?"

I give the man the address for St. Dymphna's. "It's really important that it arrives at seven P.M. No earlier, okay? I know this is going to sound ridiculous, but this is a matter of life and death."

"I gotcha, lady, pizza can be like that. Eighteen ninety-nine. You want to put it on a card?"

"Cash. The guy who's getting it is a good tipper. It's for Mark."

"Got it. Mark. The church. Seven P.M."

"Okay, and . . . thank you."

"Sure."

The phone clicks off.

"You are quite tenacious, no?"

That voice. The voice in my head when I woke up. A German accent.

I turn to find a short man in a white lab coat, dark slacks, and sneakers. His gray hair is shaggy, and he's wearing a yellow-and-blue checked bow tie. He's surrounded by a dozen men and women in owl masks, all holding stun sticks at the ready. But there's a sense of ease to the way he's standing, and I don't think it's the backup. His smile is impish, friendly—he's looking at me like I'm an old acquaintance he ran into at the train station.

"Astrid, we have not been formally introduced," he says. "I am Dr. Felix Vogt."

"Why am I here?" I ask.

He smiles again, but now there's something sad underneath the surface of it. "I am afraid I am not at liberty to divulge that."

"What can you divulge, then?"

He puts his hands behind his back and strolls toward the edge of the roof, looking out over the vastness of the ocean. "Your timing is impeccable. You were to be let out tomorrow."

"Out?"

He turns and smirks. "Not out of the prison. Out of solitary. You beat us to it!"

I look around the roof, at the men and women waiting to take a piece out of me, probably for what I did to Godfrey. "What happens now?"

"First, consequences," he says.

A lump forms in my throat. I'm about to ask what that means when there's yelling and grunting from the hatch. Godfrey is pulled up by another owl, his hands zip-tied behind his back. Vogt walks over and leans into the man's ear. His words are lost on the wind, but as he speaks, Godfrey's body slackens—first the tension disappears from his shoulders, then his legs get wobbly.

"Não, por favor," he says.

No, please.

Vogt simply shrugs at him, then puts his hands behind his back and wanders over to me. "Actions have consequences. Surely you understand that. So must the guards. Phones must be stowed at the beginning of the shift."

He nods to the owls holding Godfrey, who drag the man over to the edge of the roof and, with no hesitation or cere-mony, toss him over. Godfrey screams, and unfortunately, the wind isn't enough to cover up the sound of a sickening *thud*.

I walk to the edge of the roof, not even caring that some-one might send me tumbling over, and look down. The fall wasn't enough to kill him, but one leg is lying at a ninety-degree angle, and one of his arms is folded underneath him. He writhes there, looking up. I wonder if he sees me.

Vogt claps his hands. He's giving "enthusiastic camp coun-selor" energy right now. "You asked me what happens next. Now we enter the next step of the process."

I can't take my eyes off Godfrey. Down there and suffering.

Actions have consequences.

"And what's the next step?" I ask.

"Come," he says, offering me his hand. "How about we go get you a meal? Something clean to wear? A proper shower. With soap."

I look at that hand.

And wonder what he really has in store for me.

For a moment I consider flinging myself off the side of the building. Whatever it is they want, they're keeping me alive for it. This is a ruse, it has to be, because nothing in this world comes for free, especially in a place like this.

But no, I'm not giving them the satisfaction.

I don't take lives anymore.

Not even my own.

And clearly, it's not like the fall can kill me.

Maybe I just think I deserve to suffer a little more, down there with Godfrey.

I don't take Vogt's hand, but I do follow him toward the hatch.

MARK

Lower East Side
Now

Their footsteps announce them. The way the sound carries in this place, there wasn't much hope of covering them. They sweep into the room, sticking to the edges.

As expected.

There are eight of them. Four on either side, in cover formation.

They don't communicate verbally, but I catch the occasional hand sign in the tiny amounts of light; the orange button of the coffee maker, the yellow security light trickling in from the hallway.

It strikes me, in this moment, the level of serenity I feel.

This could be a triggering moment. How many times I've been crouched with a weapon in my hand, waiting to attack. That moment before the first bullet slices the air and the mayhem begins.

Back in the day, when I was at my peak, they'd all be dead before any of them saw me.

Now, even not wanting to be that person, even understanding how important it is they don't pursue Lucia—I don't feel that same urge. My recovery doesn't often get stress-tested. Most of my days are spent watching movies and talking to a cat.

And here I am, feeling a real clarity of purpose. More important, adrenaline isn't crackling like electricity in my fingertips. I feel no desire to play god.

Which speaks to the work I've done in recovery.

That'll be nice to unpack at the next meeting.

Right now, it's time to work.

Once the team has moved all the way in, one of the men holds out a closed fist at eye level, signaling the team to hold. They expected to find us and they're trying to figure out what's up. This is probably the end of the first wave.

I move myself into position, behind the steel-plated alcove I installed in the corner. I grip the paintball gun in my right hand, and stick my left pinkie and ring fingers in my mouth.

We've all drilled this, but Booker and me a lot more lately, because if Valencia was going to bring Lucia to the meetings, we needed to be ready. We based this on kuş dili, a whistling language developed in remote mountain regions of northern Turkey. A way for people to communicate over vast distances, since whistles carry farther than shouts.

The language has fallen out of use thanks to cell phones. But the idea of it—communicating commands to each other based on changes in pitch and melody—seemed like a fun thing to do. Booker suggested we learn a more obscure language, like Xhosa or Asturian, but you never know when someone else is a polyglot.

I blow between my fingers, giving the whistle that means *Go*.

Before the strike team can locate the source of the sound, Booker and I pop up from behind the alcoves and fire. We aim for faceplates, green paint slapping and spattering against them. The paintball guns aren't super accurate, but we hit more than we miss. With their vision impeded, they don't want to fire in the confusion and risk hitting one another.

Someone yells out, "Can't see!"

I watch through my own night vision as they start yanking off their faceplates.

Once enough of them have taken off the masks, I give the whistle for Booker to flip down the shade setting on his goggles, and I do the same.

Then I click the remote in my pocket to engage the eight-thousand-lumen lights I installed in the ceiling. That's about eight times brighter than car headlights. Even through the highly polarized lens, I have to squint a little.

But I can still see.

And they can't.

They're clamping their hands over their faces, screaming. A sizzling heat fills the room—not sure how long these are going to last before they burn out, but better to move quick.

The two of us come out of our hiding spots. Booker wields the shotgun like a surgeon. The rubber slugs send the mercenaries flying, like they were struck by massive, invisible fists. They'll walk away with some broken ribs, but they'll live.

As Booker works, I start swinging, feeling the baton spin like it's an extension of my hand, snapping it at knees and elbows and shins. We work our way through them from either side of the room.

A few of the mercenaries fire off shots as they attempt to get their bearings, the sound deafening in the space, but we're moving so fast they can't make out friend versus foe. As we go, we pick their weapons up, brace one end against the floor, and drive our heels into them, doing our best to render them unusable.

I think we're making good headway when there's a blast simultaneous with a slug slamming into my back, throwing me forward.

There's that second wave.

The vest stopped it, but it's still like getting hit with a bat. I use the momentum to roll myself forward and onto my feet. The alcove is too far; I opt for the stairwell that'll lead me up into the church. Bullets chew the doorframe behind me as I struggle to pull air into my flattened lungs.

Booker gives me a whistle for: *I'm good.*

I glance around and he's back behind his alcove, three men looking for their own cover. I kill the high-intensity lights and give him the whistle that'll let him know I'm headed upstairs.

I hate to leave Booker, but one of us needs to stay and watch the hatch, and I may as well take this as an opportunity to clear out the rest of the building. I bound up the stairs, not bothering to hide the weight of my footfalls. As I reach the corner I come around low.

No one on the other side.

I do the same at the next corner, and there's a mercenary waiting for me.

He's got his gun out and up, but I come in low, and he doesn't have time to readjust. I slip my body between his legs and push up as hard as I can, sending him sprawling. He fires into the ceiling. Once he's on his back I snatch the gun out of his hands, unload it, and throw it down the stairs behind me, then kick him hard across the jaw.

Once I know he's out of commission I head up the stairs, into the church.

The room is dim, the place mostly stripped. The pews are broken and moldering. Jesus hangs from his spot on the cross, looking down at me with that same judgmental gaze he always has.

Why I like to avoid this part of the building.

I take the remote out of my pocket—the one I didn't want to have to use. Maybe it's time to use it. I flash the lights downstairs three times, to let Booker know to put on his gas mask, and as I'm pulling mine off my belt, a soft voice echoes through the room.

"The Pale Horse."

I turn to find a rakishly handsome man, with wavy dark hair and a thick beard, standing near the vestibule. He's outfitted in tac gear, too, but his sleeves are rolled up, showing off intricately tattooed forearms, and he has several stylish bracelets around each wrist.

"Not anymore," I tell him. "I go by Mark now."

The man smiles and swaggers forward, speaks in a soft,

lyrical brogue. "Isn't this the craic. I had hoped that one day our paths would cross."

"And you are?"

He squints a little, like he's offended I don't know him straightaway. But then he offers a mocking little genuflection. "The name is Balor."

Ah.

I do know him. Or at least *of* him. An Irish hitter, ex-IRA gone freelance. He has a reputation for being brutal, effective, and flexible. Every professional has a code—things they will and will not do. "No women, no kids"—that kind of thing. His code, from what I hear, is driven purely by how much he's getting paid.

Still, it's worth a shot, to barter for a little professional courtesy.

"The group I'm with . . . there's a baby on the playing field," I say. "Three weeks old. Call off your men. Let the rest of them go. We can make this about you and me."

He tilts his head, then looks around the church, like he's considering it. Then he shrugs. "They told me to clear the room, so we clear the room."

Okay. So it's like that.

"Let me ask you something," I say. "Balor. That's an Irish mythological beast, right? A giant with one eye?"

"So you *do* know me," he says, a hint of reverence in his voice, which he tries to hide, failing miserably.

"Just, an interesting choice of name. You're, what, five foot seven, tops? Compensating for something, are we?"

Even from across the room I can see his eyebrow twitch. I

hit a nerve because I was aiming for it. If we're going to throw down, I want him angry.

Angry means stupid.

"Oh, that's grand," he says. "A comedian, are ye?"

"I am pretty funny, yeah. So now that we're friends, why don't you tell me where Astrid is."

He takes a few steps toward me. "I cannae tell you who Astrid is. I was hired to come here and kill whoever received that pizza. Simple as that. Had I known I was going to run into you . . ."

I put up my hands and wave them. "Surprise!"

"I've heard the stories. That you laid down arms. That you left the life." His lips twist into a condescending smirk. "Why?"

"That what you want to do? Have a philosophical discussion?"

He shakes his head. "Nah, but you can't blame a guy for being curious, can ye?" He pats his chest and points to me. "C'mon. Pro to pro. What's the story here? We're all going to the same place in the end, so what difference does it make."

I sigh deep. "Just got tired of killing."

"Naaaaw," he says, drawing it out. "You didn't. A blade doesn't stop being a blade when it's not drawing blood. You were looking for something. What did you find?"

I want to tell him: a little bit of serenity.

But I've been falling short on that recently.

"Right now the only thing I want to find is my friend," I tell him.

"You're being evasive," he says, his voice taking on a mocking tone. "Why is that? Is this really so hard to talk about?"

"Why do you care?"

"It's a simple question," he says, taking a few more steps toward me, his hands spread, palms up, almost like he's trying to mimic the position of Christ on the cross.

He's trying to distract me, get closer to me. I take a step back, to maintain some distance. But there's something else, too, in his voice. It's not so much a yearning, but certainly a genuine curiosity.

"Because I don't want my life to be defined by the mistakes I've made," I tell him. "Because I want to be better."

"But you were the best." He chuckles. "Besides me, of course. Giving up, what kind of difference does that really make? You think you can atone for the things you've done?"

"You know what?" I hit the button on the remote, take my gas mask and put it on. "Don't really have time for this."

As I'm getting my mask into place I realize he's putting on his own.

The guys downstairs, they were scrubs. This is the kind of person who, if I had the choice, I would never want to throw down with.

But it looks like I don't have a choice.

The adrenaline comes in now, doing its job, but the way I want it to.

Back in the day I treated it like gasoline that I'd throw on the raging fire at the dark part of my soul, but now I see it for what it is: a tool to slow down time, give me a chance to respond.

To move the energy around.

He comes at me, hands up, testing the distance. No weapon. He wants to see what I'm made of, and through that, what he's made of. I meet his stance, circle him a little. He's shorter than me, but he's hammered out of rock. I don't train the way I used to, but ten minutes of jumping rope every day keeps me light on my toes.

Still, out of practice is out of practice; I nearly don't see his foot as it snaps toward the side of my head. God he's fast. I pull back at the last second and it narrowly misses my mask. As he resets himself I throw a low kick at his standing leg, which sends him stumbling back a little.

He nods, impressed.

We move toward each other, waiting for the other to strike. I think he's going for the same thing I am. To get the mask off. He doesn't know exactly why I'm wearing it, but he knows I put it on, so it must be important.

He lunges, throwing a flurry of blows at me. I keep my arms up and absorb a few shots, hand a few back to him.

After about a minute of this, passing punch-and-kick combinations like tennis balls, it's clear that we're pretty evenly matched. I'm getting winded. It's hard to breathe through the mask, but he's not slowing down.

His mask is fogging up, though, whereas mine isn't, so I go for a few high punches, nearly over his head, trying to draw his attention as north as I can, before I throw out a fast kick, hooking around his calf and pulling him forward, spreading his stance and throwing him off balance.

Before I can reach his mask, he snaps an elbow up and catches me on the chin, nearly dislodging mine. Then he reaches his hand behind him, probably for a weapon. Tired of this dance.

My body reacts the second his hand moves. I dive toward him, knocking him clean off his feet. The two of us tumble to the floor and then we're just grappling, trying to protect our faces while attacking the other one's head. He's smaller than me, but he's fast, and he's strong.

The point now is to survive.

When I finally get my hands around the bottom of his mask, I feel a bit of relief as I'm able to pull myself back and rip it from his face. A feeling which is very quickly extinguished when I taste the air and realize he got mine off, too.

Balor takes a deep breath, searching for some kind of scent. "So what's in the air?" he asks.

"Three-quinuclidinyl benzilate," I tell him. "Screws with cognitive function. Should induce a fit of delirium and halluci-nations."

He nods. "I know what BZ is. In a space this big, it should take a few hours to really take effect, though."

"Fun fact. I meant to use this on a job years ago and didn't realize that. But I've learned more about it since then. I put sodium bicarbonate in the mix. It increases the absorption rates of most drugs. Plus, I used a *lot* of BZ." I wave my hand around the space. "Let's see how it goes."

Balor's eyes widen. "I guess now it's a matter of which one of us goes crazy first?"

"Not really," I tell him, removing a single-use injector from my pocket, which I stab into my neck. I press the button, feel a small prick, and toss it at his feet. "Seven-MEOTA. Counter-acts BZ. Sorry, I've only got the one."

Balor scrambles for it, turning it over in his hands to see if there's a way for him to extract another dose, but it's already cashed.

"Bold," I tell him. "You don't know where I've been."

I can feel it now, a dull thrum at the back of my skull, something dark fluttering at the edge of my vision, but if I'm lucky, the antidote will work and I'll be fine. Balor, meanwhile, doesn't look so hot—his eyes are darting around the room, like the space is suddenly filled with insects and he's trying to locate them in the dwindling light.

"Not really worth interrogating you," I tell him. "Figure if you don't know where Astrid is, you're useless to me. I want you to know that this whole thing here wasn't personal, and if you decide to make it that, that's going to be a *you* problem. Just because I quit doesn't mean I'm nice. And when you speak to your employer, let them know I'll see them soon."

He shakes his head, like he's trying to dislodge something, and offers me a serene smile. Then he removes a remote from his pocket.

The second I see it, I don't even wait—I run for the door.

Remotes are never good.

The first explosion hits as I'm making my way down the stone steps of the church, nearly knocking me off my feet. I stumble a bit but manage to stay upright, making it onto the street. The SUVs the mercenaries arrived in look empty, but I'm not waiting around to find out if they have any more men stationed outside.

And if they're smart they'll have at least one sniper on the building next door, so I tuck my head and sprint toward the corner, staying low against the line of parked cars. My suspicion is confirmed when a patch of pavement next to me explodes, the shards of rock close enough to bounce off my leg.

I keep running. Hear the crack of two more shots, but don't feel them land. Probably good that I can hear them.

It's the one you don't hear that kills you.

I make it around the corner, to some degree of relative safety, and look for the nearest subway station as three more explosions thump the humid night sky.

St. Dymphna's is burning.

The people I love may or may not be safe.

I don't know where to go or what to do next.

And yet, still, all I can think is:

Where the hell are you, Astrid?

▌▌

Now we gotta make the best of it, improvise,

adapt to the environment, Darwin, shit

happens, I Ching, whatever man, we gotta

roll with it.

—Vincent, Collateral

ASTRID

Midtown Manhattan
Thirteen Years Ago

The man sitting behind the lobby desk—retired cop probably, solid but growing soft in the middle, a buzz cut that's
more economical than fashionable—he's trying. He really is.
But the dress I'm wearing isn't leaving a single thing to the
imagination.

Still, I admire the intensity with which he's holding eye
contact, visibly struggling to keep his gaze from dropping
down past my collarbone.

"You're new," he says.

"That's right," I tell him, the strands of my black wig tick-
ling my face.

He nods, then stands up from the desk, wincing a little, fa-
voring his left knee.

"You okay?" I ask.

"Old football injury," he says.

I wonder if that's true, or if he did it doing something more mundane and wants to impress me. As he makes his way around the desk, I tell him, "You can go across the street to CVS and get a ten-dollar brace. They make a world of difference."

"Huh," he says, rooting around in his blazer. "Never thought of that. Thanks."

He comes out with a gray key card and walks me to the elevator. I step inside and he leans in and swipes it, then stabs the button marked P and steps back. He keeps his hand in the door, contemplating something.

"Word of advice?" he asks.

My face must go dark at that, but he puts his hand up, a gesture meant to show some deference. "Not like that. I got nothing against what you do. Just . . ." He glances up and raises an eyebrow. "Be careful with that one."

I don't have to ask what he means.

"I'm a big girl," I tell him.

He nods, steps back, and lets the doors close.

My breath catches in my chest, for just a moment.

That was kind of him.

But it also wasn't. Because he knows what's going to happen, and he's letting me go up there anyway.

The elevator is so opulent it has a padded bench. Just in case you can't bear a minute without sitting. Or maybe just a lot of old people live here. It reaches the penthouse and I step out, directly into a gorgeous apartment—floor-to-ceiling windows with a spectacular view of the Empire State Building, a grand piano in the center of the room, soft music filling the space. Mozart, maybe?

And the man I'm here to see: Chester Taft.

If it weren't for the resting-asshole face, he might be handsome. He's barefoot, in slacks and a white button-down shirt, which is open, revealing a bit of a gut hanging over his belt line. He's standing at a bar, pouring himself a glass of what looks like whiskey. He glances over at me and asks, "Where's Kate?"

"She's sick, sir," I tell him. "Mistress Christa thought you might like me."

"You tell Mistress Christa to warn me next time that she's sending someone new," he says. "I don't like surprises."

He puts down the decanter and saunters over, not offering me a drink. He stands a few feet away, taking me in, and he looks pleased by what he sees.

"I assume Mistress Christa told you what I like," he says.

"Yes, sir."

The word *sir* feels caustic in my mouth. Most men like Chester Taft—head of a real estate empire he likes to pretend he built, but really it was bequeathed to him by his father—they like to be warriors in the boardroom and delicate little crying babies in the bedroom. They need to give up control, maybe to make the rest of it seem sweeter.

But Taft is a sadist.

He wants a good little submissive who is going to listen to what he says and do even more. It's telling, that he doesn't ask me about safe words, and I don't expect him to, either.

"Go to the bedroom. Strip. Get in the bed. Wait for me. I'll be in when I'm ready for you."

"Yes, sir," I tell him.

He nods toward the bedroom and crosses over to the kitchen. I make my way down the hallway, toward the bedroom. I pass a study and a massive marble guest bathroom and two closed doors—one of them presumably the bedroom of his teenage daughter, who is currently out of town with her mother.

Men like Chester Taft should never be fathers.

The bedroom is sparse. A bed that seems slightly bigger than a king, maybe a custom job, covered in a cream-colored throw. Other than that, there's a dresser and a beautiful view of the city, the lights in the windows of the buildings around us like a starscape against the night sky. The only other door in the room leads to the master bathroom.

I go straight to the dresser and put down my clutch, then take out the preloaded syringe. Hold it up to the light. I give it a little tap and squirt to make sure there are no air bubbles. The concentration of oleander inside should kill him quickly, while making it appear he had a heart attack. I don't want to add a pulmonary embolism to the mix. That could make a coroner look a little closer and ask questions.

The hardest part is going to be choking him out without causing any noticeable injury, so I can get him onto the bed and inject him in some hard-to-find location—between the toes is best. Just a matter of getting my forearm wrapped around his neck and cutting off the blood flow long enough to render him unconscious. Which sounds easy enough, as long as he doesn't fight back too hard.

And all they'll know at the front desk is he called in a sex worker who didn't show an ID. The guard might get fired. I feel bad about that, but only a little.

Just as I'm scouting the room, figuring out the angles, thinking of the best way to do this, the lights go out.

I'm wondering if this is part of whatever scenario he likes to play out, when I hear him mutter "What the fuck" from somewhere deep in the apartment. I look out the window, at the building across from us, and the lights are still on. Must be confined to this building.

I stash the syringe and hear a crash from the front of the apartment.

Shit.

I kick off my heels—they'd be useless to move in—and head toward the entrance to the bedroom, where a man in tactical gear and helmet is coming at me, holding up a hand-gun.

"Hands, now," he barks.

There's yelling from inside the apartment. More commands.

A dull *thud*, like someone dropped a watermelon.

A cry of pain.

The man glances back, and I have to make a split-second decision here, so I throw my hand out, pushing the gun offline and away from me while gripping the barrel. When it fires it roars in the confined space, but with my hand on it, the chamber can't slide to rerack another round. I yank the gun down and toward my body, snatching it from his grasp, breaking his trigger finger in the process.

He screams in pain. I throw a push kick into his chest, sending him sprawling, then hop over him and make my way to the living room, gun up. It's maybe not the smartest move, diving into the fray, but there are no other exits from this apartment, other than a service entrance behind the kitchen.

I have no idea what I expected to find in the living room, but I thought I had a decent chance of fighting my way out of this.

Instead I find six men in similar gear, with Taft on his knees at the center, blood streaming from a nasty gash on his face. They all look up at me as I enter, and I spin back behind the doorway, to give myself some cover. If I come in low, I might be able to pick off one or two of them, but there's no way I'm making it out of here alive.

A voice says, "Everyone stand down. Miss, I need you to toss the gun across the room and come out with your hands up. No one's going to hurt you."

"How do I know that?"

"You don't, really. But you're outgunned. So let's start with a conversation and see what we can figure out, okay?"

Maybe they think I'm just a call girl. Maybe they think if they throw enough cash at me, I'll go away and pretend this never happened. Maybe I can talk my way out of this.

It's better than a shoot-out.

I toss the gun. It clatters across the hardwood floor.

"Excellent," the voice says. "Now please come out, hands raised high."

I step around the doorway and there's another man, in a white button-down shirt and dark slacks, with a bulletproof vest strapped to his chest. He's dark-skinned, with long, wavy black hair. He's handsome, but that kind of handsome that makes him dangerous, because he knows how he looks.

"There you are," he says. "What's your name?"

I don't answer.

He puts his hand to his chest. "I'm Ravi. The man I sent in after you, is he alive?"

As if on cue, the man comes stumbling down the hallway, cradling the hand with the broken digit. He pushes past me and says, "Bitch broke my finger."

"That's on you," Ravi says.

Instinct kicks in. "Oh, c'mere you big baby," I tell him.

Everyone stops and looks at me. I lead the man with the broken finger into the kitchen as everyone watches, more curious than worried. Maybe this will win me some points. I pull on handles until I find what I'm looking for: the junk drawer. Every kitchen has one, even in a place as nice as this. I root around until I find what I need—a roll of masking tape and some chopsticks.

"Give me your hand," I say.

He eyes me suspiciously. Ravi, standing behind him, shrugs. "Do it."

I think he wants to see what's going to happen next.

The man looks back at him before turning his attention to me. I take his injured hand, his pointer finger bent at an awkward angle, and say, "Deep breath. I'm going to count to three."

He nods and inhales.

"One . . ." I say, and then yank his finger, resetting the bone.

"God damn it," he yells.

I break the chopsticks in half and use them as a splint, putting one piece on either side of his finger, then wrap it with the tape—snug, but not too snug.

"There," I say. "Until you can get it looked at."

Ravi pats the man on the shoulder. "Head back to the office with the rest. We'll talk about this later." Then he turns to me. "There's a study down the hall. Why don't we go there. Have a drink and talk."

Without seeing too many other options, I nod, then go to the study, pick the comfiest chair—a plush wingback—and sit. The room is full of books and I wonder how many of them Taft has actually read; they look more like showpieces, with heavy binding and gilded edges. Ravi goes to the bar, looking through the bottles, until he mutters, "Holy shit."

"What?" I ask.

He holds up a bottle. "Twenty-year Pappy Van Winkle. This is something, like, three thousand a bottle. Would you like some?"

"Sure."

He grabs two crystal tumblers, doses out generous pours, and hands me one, then sits in the seat across from me. He leans forward and tilts his glass to mine. We tap them together. Then we both take long sips. The whiskey is soft on my tongue, and not nearly as impressive as I imagined.

Ravi makes a face and breathes through his teeth. "What do you think?"

"Good," I tell him. "Not three-thousand-dollars good."

"Agreed, a bit of a letdown," he says. He places the glass on the table next to him. "So, I bet you're wondering what's going on. We are, too. I'm going to ask you a few questions, and if I feel satisfied with your answers, I'll let you ask some questions."

"No deal."

"What do you mean, no deal?"

"We're going to start with you telling me who you are, and what you're doing."

He nods. "You're not a prostitute, I'm guessing."

I give him a little shrug.

He smiles. "Okay. I like you. I told you my name is Ravi. I represent an . . . organization that has a vested interest in Mr. Taft. We've been surveilling him for the last few weeks."

"Regarding?"

"Some business deals with the Saudis."

"Ah," I say. "You've got the place wired for sound. And video. You saw me take out the syringe. That's why you came in. You need him alive." I take another sip. "So you're more than aware that he's been beating the shit out of sex workers. Maybe you thought I was trying to protect the other girls? Then you saw I could handle myself and figured there was more to the story."

Ravi purses his lips, trying not to show that he's impressed, but struggling to keep it under wraps. "I'd say that's where I'm at, yeah. Who is Taft to you, exactly?"

The full truth?

I have a friend who works the NYPD's sex crimes unit.

Every now and again she thinks they have someone dead to rights and it turns out they're too powerful to pursue. So she calls me. Those men tend to have heart attacks soon after.

Such a funny quirk of the world.

Mistress Christa signed off, too—she saw the state of her girls, realized it was getting worse, and knew the cops would be no help. They never are.

Case in point.

"If you were surveilling him, then you knew exactly what he was doing, and you just stood back and watched," I tell him. "That's about giving me the measure of you."

Ravi grimaces a little. "The things he's tied up in, they affect the world on a global scale . . ."

"Right. Who cares if he knocks around some prostitutes, then uses his money and power to skirt the law?"

Ravi sits back, eyebrows furrowed. He looks like he wants to defend himself, even opens his mouth to start. Then he takes a deep breath and smiles. "Army? Wait, no . . . Special Forces. That where you got the medical training?"

"I was a Girl Scout."

That one earns a laugh. "I don't normally do this, but you've hit most of my boxes so far. What do you do for a living?"

"I'm a temp."

He nods. "How would you like to work for an organization that helps keep the world spinning in the right direction? You'll make a lot of money in the process."

"Like a government thing?"

"Sort of. It's called the Agency."

"So like the CIA?"

He narrows his eyes. "No, we're our own thing."

"The name isn't very imaginative, then."

"What we lack in imagination we make up for in effectiveness," he says. "Since we were founded in the 1940s, the world could have ended six times. We stopped it every time. We're not always perfect but we do the best we can. We go after the bad guys. The ones who really matter. Normally I research and recruit for this position, but you've deeply impressed me."

"What position is that?"

"The tip of the spear."

"You want me to be an assassin?"

"You clearly have no problem killing people," he says. "And I think you understand that sometimes people just need killing."

I think back to that ranch home in Albuquerque.

"Sometimes they do, yeah," I tell him.

"The only thing is, if I'm going to hire you, I need to know your name."

"Astrid."

"Astrid," he says. "Then I already know your handle. We still need to talk some more, look into your background, see if this is the right fit."

"And if it's not?"

Ravi smiles and shrugs. "You can say no. And then you can regret it in the time it takes your body to hit the pavement outside."

He says it like it's a joke, but I also suspect he is not joking. He stands and offers me his hand. "Let's go back to my office. Order some takeout. Talk for a bit. What do you think?"

I stand. "What would my handle be, then?"

"Azrael."

Hmm. The Angel of Death.

Ever since I left the army and came back to the world, I've struggled to find my place in it. I knew I could do things other people couldn't. But the buttoned-up world of law enforcement didn't seem the right fit. I can't tolerate the corruption, the injustices. I've barely been able to make ends meet, putting my skills as a medic to work as a black-market trauma surgeon.

The problem I've had, really, is that the only person I trust is myself.

Not to say I trust Ravi.

And I am certainly not going to forget all the women he turned a blind eye to over the last several weeks. One day, I'm going to make him remember that.

But something about hearing the name "Azrael" gives a little song to my soul.

It might not be *my* purpose, but it's *a* purpose.

I reach across and return the shake.

ASTRID

Somewhere near São Paulo
Two Hours Before St. Dymphna's Explodes

D r. Vogt leads me into a large, circular room. Gray and sterile and overlit to the point where there aren't any shadows. In the center of the room are six metal picnic tables, a couple of them covered with board game boxes.

Around the perimeter of the room—at ground level, and on a walkway above us—are a series of heavy dark blue doors with small security windows set into them.

There are two owls behind us. I glance at them, worried they might want revenge for Godfrey, but they appear impassive.

Vogt looks excited, like he's been waiting to show me around.

None of this is what I was expecting.

I expected to go back to my cell. Back to an unending loop of the only Dexys Midnight Runners song I can name. Being here, with people, without that damn song, feels somewhat alien. I'd gotten used to my weird little hell.

This alternative would feel welcome, if I wasn't expecting another shoe to come crashing down from the ceiling and land directly on my head.

Vogt leads me to an open cell door on the bottom level and stands aside, then sweeps his arm out, like a real estate agent presenting a dream home.

"These will be your new quarters," he says. "You may examine them, collect your clothes, and we will take you for a shower. You will have privacy, I promise. A guard will escort you to the cafeteria after. Dinner is about to start."

I want to say *thank you,* but also, I don't, so I nod at him and step inside the cell.

It's different than the one I was in. The floor is flat and the cot isn't slanted. On the bed, which sports a slightly thicker mattress, is a folded pink jumpsuit, a pair of slippers, and a thin towel. The cell has the same sink-toilet combo as the other one did, but this one has toilet paper.

I've never been so thankful to see toilet paper.

I take my stack of clothing and step out. Dr. Vogt smiles at me and says, "I'm sorry, I have something I must attend to quickly. The guards will escort you and I will come see you shortly."

He turns and hustles away, leaving me with another owl— this one a woman. She nods her head toward a door on the other side of the room. I follow her to it and then she stands to the side like a sentry. Inside is a large room with several showerheads. There's also an alcove with a bench, a mirror, and a small assortment of cleaning supplies—including a bin of off-brand tampons.

I peel off my wet clothes and toss them in a corner, hoping to never see them again. When I'm naked I realize I didn't even check to see if there are cameras, but at this point, I truly don't care. I do turn and look in the mirror, twisting myself around, so I can see the scar on my back.

Sometimes I need to remind myself that it's there.

Mostly it's just that I never want to forget.

I turn on one of the showerheads. The soap and hotel-sized bottles of shampoo and conditioner are not of any real quality, but they're better than nothing.

After I'm clean, finally clean for the first time in a month, I towel down and get dressed. There's a pair of underwear and a sports bra folded into the jumpsuit. The cheap slip-on shoes are a touch too big, but they'll do.

Fresh clothes. Clean skin. I feel like a new person.

I step outside and without looking at me, the owl leads me through the room, into a long corridor, then into another building. The layout seemed simple from the outside—three main buildings connected by covered tunnels, but the inside is slightly confusing. There are more twists and turns than I would have expected. That might be deliberate, to keep the inmates from garnering a good understanding of the space.

The woman leading me has an angry red dot on her forearm, like she was injected with something. Maybe some kind of inoculation? I'm pretty sure Brazil doesn't require any special vaccinations . . .

Before I can truly contemplate that, I smell the food.

The cafeteria is a large space, with long rows of tables, half full of inmates. A mix of pink and blue scrubs, which at first glance I thought might differentiate sex, but they don't; the crowd seems to be all men, and there are some wearing pink. There are also a dozen owls stationed at various points around the room.

A few faces turn to look at me.

Curiosity at the fresh meat.

Others can't be bothered. They just hunker down with their trays.

One of them I recognize right off. Jonathan Wampler. A handsome Navy SEAL in his midtwenties. Square jaw, piercing blue eyes. Last I saw him, in an article in the *New York Times*, he had leaked classified documents related to collusion between the U.S. and Russian governments over weapons. He was court-martialed but disappeared before sentencing. He was presumed dead.

Now he's here, in a blue jumpsuit.

He doesn't know me. He just throws me a glance and looks down at his tray.

Another man seems to give me the stink eye; an older Black man with a weathered face. I don't recognize him—maybe he recognizes me?

A voice calls out, "Hey!"

I turn to find a face I know, and never expected to see again.

Chen Yumei.

She's in a pink jumpsuit, ten feet away from me, her fists shaking, body vibrating with rage. She's holding on to a cart that has small paper cups on it.

I haven't started my eighth step, my list of people to whom I need to make amends, but she's going to be on it.

My heart leaps into my throat, where the apology gets stuck.

How could I even apologize for what I did to her?

Six years ago. Yumei was a Chinese activist, organizing striking workers at a technology plant in Shenzhen. She was small, in her twenties, but her voice carried, and she was rallying enough people that the Chinese Communist Party got worried. As the heat on her intensified, she fled to the United States, to avoid being disappeared. She settled under an assumed name with family in San Francisco and took a job waiting tables.

The problem for her was, the Agency was trying to make nice with the CCP at the time, and they asked for her back. They saw her as a sleeping threat, biding her time until she could get her hands around another megaphone.

They needed her gone.

So I tracked her down, drugged her, and dropped her off with some stern-faced men at a waiting boat. And I was sloppy because I let her see my face. I didn't think it would make a difference.

It was one of those jobs I didn't feel good about. She was a force for good in the world, but back then, I was a tool for the Agency, and according to them, this was about keeping tensions from boiling over with China. It was about keeping the economy flowing.

I did my job.

As if I could explain that to her.

I put my hands out, searching for something to say. "Listen . . ."

She steps toward me until we're almost nose to nose. "I've been through hells you couldn't imagine. Bounced from place to place until I wound up here. They have tried so goddamn hard to break me. And some days, I wish I would. One of the things that got me through it was the hope I would see you again."

"I . . ."

She throws a wide hook at me. The kind of punch a drunken idiot throws outside a bar. I step back, get my arm up, and block it. Look around the cafeteria, wondering if I'll get some kind of help here, but the owls are standing stone still, watching. The other inmates are seated calmly, every conversation stopped, every gaze pointed in our direction.

No one's going to step in.

Maybe this is payback for Godfrey.

Yumei throws a clumsy kick. I step aside, just in time to turn into another hook. It doesn't land with a ton of force or precision, but there's just enough to stagger me. The girl I met all those years ago wasn't capable of this. I guess a few years in prison will do that.

And it's my fault.

My fault that she's here. My fault that she got ground down into this, from a bright-eyed activist to the wild, feral woman in front of me.

She comes at me again, throwing more blows. I dodge some, block others. Every opening she leaves me is clear as day, like she's offering them on a platter. I lose count of the ways I could end this.

But I can't. Can't strike back. Can't swing.

I could destroy her with a few flicks, but I already destroyed her.

Which leaves me to, what?

Take the beating?

Is that what I deserve? Does the pain balance the scales a little here?

I stop working so hard to get out of the way. Let her land some harder blows. Wondering at what point someone is going to intervene, or if she's just got free rein to kill me. I keep a close eye on her hands, in case she pulls out a shank. I don't think she's carrying one, but you never know. That's the point of a shank. You're not supposed to see it until it's delivered two dozen puncture holes to your stomach.

A harsh whistle splits the air.

In my peripheral vision, inmates drop their heads forward onto the tables, placing their hands behind their heads. I drop to the ground, but Yumei isn't playing along. She's looking around, desperate, angry.

"No," she yells. "I'm not done."

But she doesn't look poised to attack me now.

She looks scared, eyes darting around the space like a frightened animal.

I feel compelled to help her. To do something. I owe her that.

Two owls come over, grab her by the arms, and drag her off, kicking and screaming.

We listen until the screams stop.

And then it's over, like nothing happened. The inmates pick up their heads and go back to talking. Part of me wants to run after Yumei. Rip her free from the guards. Apologize. Carry her out of here.

And go . . . where?

I'm HALTing. The AA acronym for hungry, angry, lonely, and tired. It's when you're most likely to relapse, and since I am currently all four of those things—most of all, angry, at myself—the best thing I can do is try to fix one and hope it helps.

So I walk to the self-serve stations and the food looks surprisingly appetizing. I was expecting slop, and instead I find a dark brown stew with big chunks of meat, crusty bread, rice, a salad, and pudding cups. I fill some bowls and take a tray over to the nearest table. The only other occupant, down at the other end, is an older Middle Eastern man, also wearing pink, his hair and beard a pleasant gray.

I take a large spoonful of the stew and am shocked to find that it's good. Not restaurant quality, but a hell of a lot better than I could do. And best of all: no dumplings. The bread is warm and crisp on the outside, soft on the inside. The salad even has a bit of quinoa.

"Alcatraz."

I look at the man on the other end of the table. He smiles, then stands, sliding his tray down so he can sit across from me. My shoulders immediately bunch, my body going into guard mode.

"You seemed surprised," the man says. "Alcatraz served high-quality food to the inmates. The warden there believed most trouble in prisons is caused by bad food."

I've never been in prison, but I've heard enough about it. People aren't friendly just to be friendly. Usually there's a reason. And there's something about his face. Despite that easy smile, despite the grandfatherly vibe, there's something unsettling about him.

"You have every right to be nervous," the man says, picking up a spoon and taking a bite of his chocolate pudding. "This place is free of many of the stereotypes you'd associate with prison. There are loyalties and cliques, but not much dissent amongst the prisoners. Surprising, perhaps, but the people here tend to be professionals. They understand who the real enemy is."

He nods toward the guards.

"What was all that, then?" I ask, gesturing to where me and Yumei faced off. "They could have stopped it right away."

"The guards will sometimes let things play out, but you're both in pink, so they had to step in."

"What does that mean?"

"Pink means valuable," the man says, tugging on his shirt. "Blue means expendable."

"Expendable how?"

"To the whims of the doctor."

Vogt.

"So," I ask, "where are we, exactly?"

The man tilts his head in surprise. "They haven't told you?"

"I've been listening to 'Come on Eileen' for the past month."

He smirks. "You went straight to solitary for a month?"

"Impressive, I know," I tell him. "I managed to get out, beat the shit out of a guard in the process. But instead of punishing me or sticking me back there, they killed him and gave me clean clothes."

I don't actually know if Godfrey is dead, but for his sake, I hope he is.

The man nods. "Their reasoning is not always entirely clear. You are in a privately funded prison. It doesn't have a name. Many of us call it the Tenth Circle. One level lower than Dante's ninth. Clever, you see? Every single person who is here, someone is paying to keep here. In my case, it is the United States government."

There's something about his face. I just can't place it. But I don't know what's polite and what's not in this setting—asking him his name or his sins might be taboo, so I keep digging for information.

"I know we're off the coast of Brazil," I tell him, "and it's probably too far to swim."

The man nods. "We are about twenty miles from the coast, and no, the swim would be quite impossible. Even without the sharks. We are on Ilha da Queimada Grande. Also known as Snake Island. It is the only natural home of the golden lancehead pit viper. The island is full of them. Even if you were to escape, you might not make it to the water's edge. They are quite deadly."

I imagine Godfrey, covered in snakes.

He took this job. He knew the risks.

Still . . .

The man looks around, glancing at the cameras in the corners of the room, the owls. "Something you may find helpful to know, as well, is that while many of the guards do not speak English, they do speak violence."

"Seems like you'd want to have some English-speaking guards," I say. "The two of us could be plotting to escape."

The man's eyes go wide, darting around the room.

"Do not use that word, in any context," he says, a little sharply. "There are microphones everywhere, picking up and recording what we say, and they use artificial intelligence technology to transcribe and scan that text, to search for troublesome phrases. A few months ago, two inmates started planning something and were caught within minutes of formulating their plans."

"Jesus," I say. "The panopticon is real."

"You will get used to it." Then he pauses. "I understand this may be an impolite question, and you may not wish to answer, but, why are you here?"

Not taboo, then.

"No one has told me anything."

"But you are a professional," he says.

Interesting. Game tends to recognize game.

"With enough red in my ledger to make guessing who brought me here an impossible task," I tell him. "Are you pro, too?"

"In a way," he says. "My name is Fahad."

And there it is.

The missing puzzle piece that snaps it together in my head and shoots a blast of frigid air straight across my soul.

He sees that I recognize him, and gives a pained, embarrassed smile.

Fahad Quraishi.

Also known as the Shiqq.

Laying eyes on him is like seeing Bigfoot. The Shiqq was pursued by the United States and Israel—hell, probably every NATO country—for decades, and thought to be responsible for orchestrating countless murders, suicide bombings, kidnappings, and assassinations.

Thought being the operative word, because he was also a ghost.

That photo I saw of him, once, during prep for an Agency op, was the only photo of him known to exist. It was grainy, taken from a distance. He was younger, getting into a car in Lebanon. He was a suspected associate of the target we were pursuing, but the operation wasn't focused on him; the Agency wasn't telling us to look for him, they were telling us to give him a wide berth.

The subtext was clear.

They were afraid of him.

He wasn't just bloodthirsty, he was brilliant, and he would jump at the chance to take out an American operative.

Then, probably around four years ago, he disappeared. No one even considered whether he was dead; he was too smart for that.

"Heavy is the head . . ." he says, but before he can finish the thought, he looks up and past me, his eyes focusing on something. "Hello, Dr. Vogt."

"Fahad, how are you feeling today?" he asks. "Are you still having trouble sleeping?"

"Always," he says. "I do enjoy the taste of the melatonin gummies you gave me, but they don't seem to be helping."

"Why don't you come by my office tomorrow," Vogt says. "I'm not sure I'll be able to get approval for something stronger, but I can try." A soft hand appears on my shoulder, which I can't help but recoil from a little. "Astrid, I'm sorry I had to leave you like that. How are you feeling after a shower and some food?"

"Am I supposed to thank you?" I ask.

"I suppose not," he says. "Would you please come with me?"

"Do I have a choice?"

"I am sorry, but you do not."

"Then don't say 'please' like it's supposed to mean something," I tell him.

He nods. "I will have someone bus your tray."

I give a look at Quraishi, but he's dropped his eyes to the remainder of his food. I get up from the stool and turn to Vogt, relieved to be away from that conversation.

I've always had a high tolerance level for people in the game. We made the choices we made for the reasons we made them. Recovery has reinforced that we don't have to be defined by our mistakes.

But Quraishi played the game without rules.

Without mercy.

He killed women and children.

That's a tough bridge to cross for me.

And it's a hell of a thing that right now he's my only friend.

As Vogt leads us through the facility, an owl follows, stun

stick at the ready. We pass through a long hallway, to a stair-case, and then into a smaller, carpeted hallway.

He leads me into a room. It's a small, tidy office. There's a shelf of books, a chair, and a large mahogany desk, on which there's a computer, and a long, neat row of penguins; some are stuffed, some are made of glued-together rocks. One is plastic, with a little winding knob on the side. He takes a seat behind the desk and gestures to a chair in front of it.

"Please," he says.

I nod at the penguins. "Hobby?"

He claps his hands together, excited to show them off. "My daughter gets them for me. She is six, obviously she could never visit, but she gives them names and asks me to send pictures of them to her. She says it is so I will not be lonely." He picks up a small plastic figurine: a cartoon penguin wearing a bright pink wool hat and scarf. "This one, incidentally, she named Astrid."

"Sweet," I tell him.

Not even lying, really. It is sweet.

The owl closes the door and stands a little too close for me to feel comfortable.

"So who's paying for my stay?" I ask.

Vogt nods. "I am not at liberty to divulge."

"What *are* you at liberty to divulge?"

He puts his hand out, palm up. "You may continue to ask questions. I may or may not be able to answer them. I have no desire to be adversarial. I had planned to explain the specific nature of the island after you'd eaten, but I assume Fahad has already done that?"

"He did. I know that if I get past the snakes I have to deal with the sharks, so, not really formulating an escape plan. Not yet at least."

"I assure you, escape would be quite difficult, and surely result in your death. That is not my desire."

"It's not?"

"If your benefactor wished for you to die, there'd be no sense in bringing you here."

"My *benefactor*," I say. "And what is the point of me being here?"

"I'm afraid, Astrid, that is not something I am at liberty to divulge."

"You keep saying that. So, what, I just sit around?"

He frowns and shakes his head. "I will tell you this. Your stay in solitary was quite valuable, and a necessary part of the deal. It has provided me with some interesting data."

"What deal? What data?"

He furrows his brow—not at liberty.

"Why 'Come on Eileen'?" I ask.

He smiles. "Because I find it quite grating."

"I didn't used to mind it," I tell him. "Of course, I'd like it if I never heard it again."

He nods. "You were able to weather all that with a fair bit of resolve."

"I was Special Forces. I can deal with a little discomfort. Why not just send someone in there to waterboard me? Peel my fingernails back? There are plenty of ways to extract information."

"I have found, in my years of doing this, that inflicting pain in pursuit of information is rarely effective," he says. "Often subjects will say whatever it is they have to say in order to bring that particular episode to a close—and what they say isn't always the truth. Anyway, those forms of torture are often perpetrated by people who are seeking to process more difficult internal feelings. I prefer gentler methods. Time, exhaustion, and frustration are all better motivators."

"Why let me out, then?"

"Because those were the terms of the deal. We are now ready to move into the next phase of your visit here."

My blood runs a little cold at that. "Next phase?"

"Yes," he says. "During this time, you will be in the general population. No more solitary. You will have access to the food. No more dumplings! That must be exciting. The dumplings are good. One of my favorite items in the cafeteria. But I wouldn't be able to eat them every day."

"Can you tell me a little more about what this next phase entails?" I ask.

"Sadly, no," he says. "That would defeat the purpose." He settles back in his chair a little, getting comfortable. "Now, I know this is a little unfair, considering I have not been able to be very forthcoming. But there is a lingering question about the phone call you made. All of our guards have their phones tracked. We know who you called. It was very clever, though sadly, not as effective in subterfuge."

"What is that supposed to mean?"

"It means that moments after the call was made, a team was dispatched. They will surveil the restaurant, follow the delivery, and eliminate whoever it is delivered to. Presumably, someone you were hoping to get a message to. You must have understood there would be consequences."

Yeah, I did. I just didn't realize they'd come to bear so fast.

"I promise you, whoever you send isn't going to like the people they find," I tell him.

"We expected as much. You wouldn't have taken such a risk. It will be led by . . ." He picks up his phone and looks at it. "He goes by Balor. Have you heard of him?"

Shit. "Yes."

"Is he good?"

Yes, very.

"He's still up against some pretty formidable folks," I tell him.

Which is what I say. But all I can think about is a strike team descending on the church. Mark, Booker, Valencia, Ms. Nguyen. Maybe they've recruited others in the interim. They're still pretty damn dangerous, even if they can't kill. And Mark has been in the process of outfitting the church with defense measures.

Except . . . it hits me like a fist to the stomach.

The baby.

Valencia will have had the baby by now. What if she brings the baby to the meeting?

"Get whoever your employer is on the phone," I tell him. "Whatever they want to know, I'll tell them, as long as you call it off."

Vogt shrugs. "I'm sorry, but given certain . . . metrics, I highly doubt that will be the case."

He nods to the owl behind me, and before I can react, a needle pricks into the side of my neck. It withdraws quickly and I put my hand to the injection site. "What the hell was that?"

"Something to make what happens next a little more comfortable."

"What . . ."

At least, that's what my brain is telling me to say. The word feels like a marble in my mouth. My head swims, and suddenly there are three swaying Vogts in front of me.

"I know it is a ridiculous thing to say in this moment, but I do not wish to harm you, Astrid," he says. "The more you resist, the harder it will . . ."

And I drop into a cold, dark lake.

MARK

Mark?"

I look up from my cardboard container of fried rice. At Ms. Nguyen and Valencia, on the couch across from me. At Booker, seated in one of the chairs he dragged out of the kitchen. The remnants of our Chinese takeout spread across the coffee table, looking as though it's been attacked by rabid dogs.

"Where were you just now?" Ms. Nguyen asks.

"Just . . . thinking. I'm good."

She knows I'm lying.

We go back to eating.

Booker showed up with the food. He was well away from the explosion; one of the mercs had slipped into the tunnel. Booker followed to subdue him, and made it a safe distance before the church blew. Ms. Nguyen and Valencia got Julio to safety and were waiting here. They know I keep a spare key with Manny, who owns the bodega on the corner, and Manny knows they're safe to give it to.

Our fallback point. The apartment isn't under my name. It's paid for in cash. No CCTV in the building, and the camera network in the neighborhood is spotty.

It's good to have something to eat. All three of us were HALTing, which means getting some food in us would even the odds in our favor a little bit.

Booker showed up moments after we got up here, and other than letting them know that the church was a smoldering heap, we haven't spoken much. We ate. I think we were all just happy that the five of us made it back in one piece.

P. Kitty hops onto the table, sniffing the remnants of food, but not making a play for any of it. I don't know if cats can eat Chinese food but I've seen him eat electrical wires, plastic, and, once, half a deck of Tarot cards, so I'm not too worried.

Ms. Nguyen gives the orange furball a scratch behind the ears, and the cat leans into it, purring hard.

"Your daddy isn't feeding you enough, is he?" she asks.

"I'm feeding him just fine," I tell her, then pluck a dumpling out of its black plastic container. "What do we know?"

Everyone looks at me expectantly. In that brief moment of silence, Lucia gives a little cry from the bedroom, where Valencia laid her down for a nap—goddamn that kid is a trouper—and we wait a second, to hear if there's more, but she falls silent.

"Astrid is alive," Booker says.

"And wherever she is," Valencia says, "she couldn't get away, or contact us directly. So she got us a message."

"The team was headed by Balor," I say, and Booker offers a low, impressed whistle. "Yeah, he doesn't come cheap. Neither did the team's gear. So we're up against someone powerful."

"You fought him?" Booker asks.

"I did, yeah."

"What was he like?"

Valencia rolls her eyes a little. "Bunch of boys, measuring dicks."

Booker shoots her a sharp look. I tell him, "He was good, and if the fight went on much longer, I would have been in trouble. And he didn't bat an eye when I mentioned Lucia and asked for a little grace. In the end I popped the BZ, then he blew the church. He couldn't have made it out. So, he's off the table for now, at least."

I leave out the part about the question he asked.

Why?

Such a small word, and I don't understand how it feels so big.

"Any ideas on who this could be, Mark?" Ms. Nguyen asks. "Did you and Astrid start the eighth step yet?"

"No, and we never really talked specifics. But look, she worked for the Agency. We could sit here, do the work, come up with a list of as many kills as we can think of that she might have been involved with, walk away with a few dozen suspects, and still be wrong."

Valencia pats the table to get our attention. "She's been held for a month and she was well enough to get us a message. So whoever has her, they're keeping her alive."

"Long time to keep someone alive if your ultimate plan is to kill them," Booker says.

"Right," I say. "So maybe she knows something and she's not giving it up."

"There's one other thing we haven't addressed yet," Ms. Nguyen says.

"What's that?" I ask.

Her voice drops. It takes on a solemn tone. "Did everyone make it out . . . intact?"

She's looking at me and Booker when she says this.

"Yeah," he says. "All good."

"Me, too," I tell them.

And the gravity in the room seems to shift, some of the weight coming off us.

Ms. Nguyen sticks a finger in the air. "Balor. Did you see a body?"

"No, I did not."

She nods. "If you didn't see a body, assume he's still out there."

"Fair," I tell her. "Anyway, we chatted a bit, and he said he didn't know who hired him. It was an exterminator gig. Go in, clear house."

"You believed him?" Booker asks.

"No reason for him to lie. So next step is, we find Astrid. Unfortunately I don't have any idea how to do that."

"She called the pizza place," Valencia says. "If we can access their phone records, we could probably trace it back. Even if we can find a region, that'll narrow it down, and we can go from there."

"What's this *we* shit?" Booker asks.

Valencia's face drops. "Astrid is family, and like you keep on saying, family ain't blood . . ."

"I know, I know," he says. "But Lucia is family, too. And she's the only one of us who can't defend herself. Mark and I will go. Not that I need the backup."

"Prick," I tell Booker, and he throws me a little wink.

"I'll stay with Valencia and the baby," Ms. Nguyen says. "It's unlikely they're going to come after us individually, but I can call on some contacts. Get us out of the city for now. I can keep her safe."

"And god help anyone who gets in your way, right?" I ask.

She frowns, pouting out her lips. "Don't be funny, Mark. I was formidable in my day."

"Hey," I tell her, leaning over and putting my hand on her knee. "I'm dead serious. There is no one else I'd trust with this."

"You'll keep us updated?" Valencia asks.

"Of course," I say. "Keep communication to a minimum. Emergency only. I don't even want to know where you end up, as long as you're safe. We need to be off the grid. In fact, trash your cell phones and pick up some burners before you go. I think Ms. Nguyen is right. We did some damage tonight, and this was a quick job. Had they known anything about us, they would have probably just launched a nuke into the church and been done with us."

"All right," Booker says. "So where does that leave us?"

I sit back heavily in the easy chair.

We need to access the pizza place's phone records. Going in there is no dice. They might have someone watching it, and anyway, what can we do? Hold someone at gunpoint and make them sit down and pull up their phone provider's website?

"What we need," I tell Booker, "is a proper hacker. You got a clean passport?"

He nods. I take out my phone, scroll through Google until I find a flight leaving for London in four hours. "We need to pick it up, then it's off to JFK. I know someone who can help."

"We can't call him?"

"We're just going to assume that any kind of communication can be intercepted. We go there in person. He's the only one I know for a fact who'll get the job done, unless one of you knows a top-level hacker in the tri-state area."

I get nothing but blank stares in return.

"London it is."

"I'm a nervous flier," Booker says.

"You can hold my hand, tough guy," I tell him. "Ms. Nguyen, you got cash?"

"Not a lot."

I go to the wall and take the poster for *Bicycle Thieves* off it, revealing the wall safe. I open it up and pull out a couple of burner phones, in plastic clamshell cases, and toss them on the chair. "One problem solved. Forgot I had these."

Then I take out stacks of cash; twenty thousand for Ms. Nguyen and Valencia, fifty for me and Booker. Should be enough.

"Don't go home," I tell them. "Get directly out of town,

find a hotel that'll take cash, stay there for a few days, then move and keep moving. Can you take the kitty?"

"Of course," Ms. Nguyen says.

"All right. Booker, let's get a cab, get that passport, and get to the airport."

"I don't like this," Valencia says.

"There's not much here to like, but what specifically?"

"Splitting up."

"Not much to be done about that," I tell her. "Saving Astrid is a priority, but keeping that baby safe is just a bit higher."

She nods, even though I know she doesn't want to.

It strikes me in that moment, to pose to them the question Balor asked to me.

Why?

Why are we doing this?

Astrid is a big girl. Going after her like this raises the likelihood that one of us is going to end up losing our sobriety in the process. The safest thing to do would be for the five of us to disappear, save ourselves, stay safe.

Astrid wouldn't blame us.

She'd probably encourage it.

I have enough money saved up we could make a decent go of it. Somewhere on the West Coast. Maybe down in Mexico.

Anywhere that's not here.

Astrid is her own person.

But I can't do that, either. She asked for help.

And that's the whole point of this process.

Hell is empty, and all the devils are here.

—ARIEL, THE TEMPEST

ASTRID

Atlantic City, NJ
Eight Years Ago

The man standing outside the door of the hotel room clocks me the moment I step off the elevator.

My stomach drops as my brain floods with dopamine. He's not supposed to be here, and that complicates things. It's supposed to be a ghost mission. In and out without being seen. The security cameras will be erased as soon as I'm done, covering the time I spent in the hotel, which underscores the power of the Agency. Casino security tends to be tighter than most places.

I push the maid service trolley toward him. The hotel is decadent art deco, gleaming gold trim on dark lilac surfaces. There's only one door on this floor. The penthouse. Amazing how often my work takes me to penthouse apartments, though at the same time, I shouldn't be surprised.

Money makes men into monsters.

Or bigger monsters than they already were.

I approach the man guarding the room in my slightly too-baggy maid's uniform, a modest black outfit I swiped out of a locker downstairs. As I get closer to the door he says, "We did not call for room service."

The hard look and heavy Russian accent are somewhat softened by the easy grin on his face. He's wearing a crisp black suit, an earpiece stuck into his left ear. He's right-handed, carrying his gun in a concealed holster on the left side of his body.

"Well, someone did," I tell him.

He puts his hand up as I reach him, bending down to inspect the cart. The only thing I'm carrying is a syringe, on a holster attached to my inner thigh.

"Need to look before I let you in," he says, glancing back and forth between me and the cart. "You know, you are a very pretty lady. Too pretty to be working at a place like this."

"Student loans," I tell him, adding a ditzy lilt to my voice.

As he examines the cart I consider my options. He doesn't think I'm a threat so his guard is down. It'd be easy enough to swoop around him and snap his neck. But then there's a body to contend with, and that would compromise the mission. I need him to move away from this door, but also buy myself a little plausible deniability.

He's a hired gun; his loyalties are to money and his life. Chances are if he gets jammed up he's going to run rather than look for revenge, because the people he works for don't take failure lightly. A loose plan formulates in my head, and before I can even sort out the pieces of it, he finishes with the cart and says, "Perhaps I can help. With these loans."

There it is.

Three loyalties, then. Money, his life, and his dick.

"Maybe . . ." I say, playing coy, "I could find us an empty room where we could . . . talk? You can wait for me down at the bar and we can have a drink first?"

He glances at the door. "Eh, nothing to worry about in this tiny shit town. Okay then."

He leans into me like he wants to kiss me, and I step back and point up. "Cameras."

"I am Sergei," he says.

"Rose," I tell him. "The bar right downstairs. Outside the elevators and past the slot machines. I'll be there in ten minutes. I can always come back here later."

He smiles the dreamy smile of a man who thinks he's about to get laid, and heads for the elevator. I make my way to the service entrance at the end of the hallway, like I'm going to drop off the cart. When the elevator doors close, I pull out my burner phone and call 911.

"There's a man at the bar at the Riverside Casino and I think he's carrying a gun," I tell them, before giving a description and hanging up. Then I crack the phone in half and dump it into the cart.

That's one problem solved. He'll be stuck dealing with the police long enough for me to finish. With that clear I head for the door of the room, behind which I'll find my target: Dmitri Kozlov.

Kozlov is the son of a Russian oligarch causing trouble for the Kremlin. We don't generally get in bed with the Russians, but apparently we're looking to win some points so we can get something else. Those conversations are above my pay grade. All I know is that the needle strapped to my leg contains a lethal mix of heroin and fentanyl, and given Kozlov's proclivity for opioids, no one will look sideways at an overdose.

I use the master key card I stole and push my way inside, careful to close the door quietly behind me. There's a long entryway, with some chairs and a massive chandelier hanging from the ceiling. Lots of marble and hard surfaces, so I walk slow, careful to keep my footsteps from echoing.

As I creep down the hallway, I strain to listen. There's the sound of talking around the corner.

The entryway opens into a living room bigger than my entire apartment, with a massive television and an assortment of comfy couches. There's a man sitting away from me, watching a movie. I don't know what it is, but Kurt Russell is in it, and he looks young, and seems to be sitting in some kind of Arctic base.

I move quietly along the back wall, breathing shallow, watching for things in my way. The television is loud enough that he can't hear me. Kurt is now arguing with a bunch of people in a room. Apparently there's an alien in there with them, or something. I don't know. Not the thing to focus on at this moment.

I make my way to the far end of the room, just to the corner of his peripheral vision. But he's absorbed in the movie, so I crouch and slip into the next room. It's a kitchen. Nicer than my kitchen. God I hate how these assholes live.

The next few rooms are empty; a large guest bathroom, a smaller bedroom. Maybe I'm going to get lucky on this and it's just Kozlov and the guy on the couch. I'll finish the gig without breaking a sweat and maybe I can go find something good to eat.

But then I hear it.

Soft weeping.

There's a bedroom to my left. I slip inside and my heart seizes in my chest.

Sitting on the bed, legs folded under her, is an Asian girl who can't be more than fifteen. She's tiny, like a bird, gaunt like she hasn't had a good meal in forever. She's in short-shorts and a midriff shirt with pink flowers across the chest, one delicate wrist handcuffed to the headboard.

She looks up at me, a storm of pain raging behind her eyes.

She doesn't need to say it.

I don't recognize her, but I recognize it. That thing inside her.

I put my finger to my lips, beckoning her to remain silent, and I step into the hallway.

My pulse roars.

A young man in a suit comes around the corner and locks eyes with me.

Everything goes silent.

As he reaches into his jacket for the gun I dash toward him, pressing it against his body. He looks at me in confusion, thrown by the maid's outfit. I slam my knee hard into his gut, and he leans forward, which allows me the positioning I need to snap his neck.

I take the gun from his hand as he falls and stride back to the living room, where the man on the couch is in the process of getting up, scrambling for his own gun. I shoot him through the eye, sending a spray of viscera across the living room, and before his body hits the ground I'm working my way back through the suite.

Two more men appear and I kill them, simple as if I waved my hand at motes of dust.

Because I am Azrael, the Angel of Death.

I find Kozlov in the back bedroom, lying on his bed, stirring at the sound but stuck in some kind of drug-induced haze. I drop the gun and remove the syringe from my thigh holster and climb on top of him, sitting on his chest, and smack him in the face.

"Who's the girl?" I ask.

"Mogu zaplatit'," he says. "Vse, Chto vy khotite."

I can pay. Anything you want.

I punch him in the face, breaking his nose.

"Who is the girl?" I ask.

"M . . . moy."

Mine.

I take the syringe and jam it into his eye. He screams as I depress the plunger. He convulses under me, so hard I fear he might buck me off him. I wonder what it is that killed him. The heroin or the needle in the brain. Ultimately, I do not care.

"Astrid."

Ravi's voice behind me.

"Astrid, what have you done?" he asks.

When I don't move, I hear the click of the gun that's now being pointed at the back of my head.

"It wasn't supposed to go down like this," he says.

I climb off Kozlov and walk toward Ravi, until the gun is pointed firmly against my chest.

"Did you know the girl was here?" I ask.

"No."

"How did you get here so quick if you didn't have cameras in here?"

He doesn't answer, which is all the answer I need.

A man in a hazmat suit, struggling to carry a large black case, pushes past us. He sets the case on the bed and flips it open.

"There might still be time to fix this," Ravi said. "We got the guy downstairs, too. It's nice to know you started things off by being clever . . ."

"What do we do?" I ask. "With the girl. Drop her at the embassy? There's got to be some kind of . . . relocation . . ."

Ravi purses his lips. "Girl's been through a thing like that, you have to wonder what would be kinder."

I stop breathing. Ravi notices it and raises an eyebrow at me.

"The Agency doesn't offer witness protection," Ravi says.

I take a step closer to him.

"She's a child," I say.

"She's not my problem," Ravi says.

"Fine," I tell him. "She can be my problem."

Ravi shakes his head. "You're showing a lot of promise, Astrid. I'm willing to get your back on this boondoggle you just handed me. But you're now walking a thin line. I need you to understand that."

"If you're really worried, I welcome you to put a bullet in my head," I tell him. "Otherwise, get out of my way."

He lingers for a second before stepping aside. I walk back to the bedroom where I found the girl. She's still sitting on the bed, but the cuff is off, at least. There's a man standing guard with his gun drawn.

"Put that away," I tell him. "And get out."

"Only Ravi can . . ."

I grab him by the collar and pull him close. "Get out now, or I will take all your teeth out. Even the ones in the back."

The threat doesn't seem to land; he simply smirks as he holsters the gun. He has a hundred pounds on me and he thinks that makes him safe. I can't do this job if the grunts look at me like a porcelain doll, and I'm already in enough trouble. So I snatch his wrist and step back as I twist it clockwise, his palm facing the ceiling and his shoulder wound on itself like a too-tight knot. He immediately drops to a knee, gasping in pain.

I increase the pressure and get close to his ear. "I'm going to give you one more chance. Leave, or we circle back to the teeth."

"I'll go," he says, grunting.

"And say you're sorry."

He makes a sound that's someplace between a sob and a laugh, so I twist harder. A little bit further and his shoulder should pop right out of the socket . . .

"I'm sorry," he says.

I let him go, and he gasps, then grabs his arm, cradling it to his chest as he stumbles out of the room.

We'll see how that plays out. Until then, I sit on the edge of the bed, careful to give the girl a little space. I know how important space can be when you're used to people taking it away from you.

"What's your name?" I ask.

She doesn't say anything. Now that I'm closer, I can see just how thin she is. That her clothing is wrinkled and dirty. Her hair hasn't been properly washed in ages. And there are angry red marks, around both her wrists . . .

I want to kill every one of those men all over again.

"Hey," I tell her. "I'm not like them. My name is Astrid. Can you tell me yours?"

"Chea," she says, her voice a whisper.

"Chea. That's a beautiful name. Where are you from, Chea?"

"Cambodia."

That makes sense. Cambodia is a hotbed for sex trafficking, thanks to a combination of weak law enforcement, crooked government officials, and poverty. Not that our hands are clean—the United States bombed it to oblivion during the Vietnam War, creating the conditions for corruption to flourish.

"Are your mom or your dad looking for you, do you think?" I ask. "Maybe I can get you back . . ."

Her eyes go wide. "Please, no. My mom . . ."

And she starts bawling, her tiny body shaking.

"Shh," I tell her. "Can I hug you?"

She bounds forward and throws herself around me, sobbing into the crook of my neck.

I'm glad she's hugging me.

The reason for that is, she can't see that I'm crying, too.

"You sure about this?" Ravi asks from the doorway.

Without looking at him, I say, "Yes."

ASTRID

The Tenth Circle
Now

Consciousness hits me like a wave. I jerk up on my cot, expecting to slide off, or to hear the eardrum-scraping strains of Dexys Midnight Runners, but instead I'm inside my new cell. The one that isn't a torture chamber. I want to say that brings with it some degree of relief, but it does not. Not really.

Because I'm still here.

I reach my hand out, try to grasp my disintegrating memories, but they slip through my fingers like sand. All I can remember is Chea. Something about Chea.

Another amends.

One I can never make.

I swing my legs down to the floor and sit for a second, let the wave of nausea pass. Don't know how long I was out. Doesn't matter, I guess.

The rec area is empty. There's an owl standing on the stairway. Probably assigned to wait for me to come out, but then again, maybe some of these other doors have drugged prisoners sleeping it off behind them, too.

He points to a set of double doors on the other side of the room, so I make my way over and push through into the blinding sunlight. It takes my eyes a moment to adjust. I'm in the area at the center of the prison.

Inmates are scattered throughout, walking in circles around a small track, using workout equipment, sitting on benches. I find a quiet corner that the sun is hitting and sit and pull my legs up to my chest, close my eyes, enjoy the warmth of it on my face. Pretend I'm somewhere other than here.

It'll have happened by now. It's got to be the next day, at least. Balor will have made it to the meeting and I have to hope that Mark and the others were able to fight him off. That the baby is okay. That they all made it out with their sobriety intact.

Do they know I'm alive?

Do I want them to know?

Whoever is doing this is clearly willing to take drastic steps to keep me here. Balor is someone I've only heard stories about, and none of them are good. Maybe they'll do the smart thing and leave me be. Get somewhere safe. Protect themselves.

At this point, if they asked me, it's what I'd tell them to do.

It doesn't matter where I go, it doesn't matter what I do, people get hurt. Godfrey must be dead by now. I hope he is.

Did the snakes get him? How much of that is my fault? I knew there would be consequences for my actions, but I didn't realize there'd be consequences for him.

And that's on me now.

All I know for sure is: whatever happens to me now is just the closing of a karmic circle.

I was always going to end up here.

Live by the blade, die by it.

I just wonder where the blow is going to come from.

And within moments, I get a sense.

Yumei is staring poison-tipped daggers at me from across the yard. It would be so easy to just walk across and sit and try to explain why I did what I did. Not that I think she'll understand, but I'm going to have to start making amends sooner or later. And if I'm probably not going to make it out of here, maybe I ought to just make the one.

That could be something.

I'm considering it, when there's a soft whirring sound, somewhere in the distance, which grows until a helicopter rises in the air, over the high crest of the wall, before banking and disappearing.

The energy of the yard shifts. People seem more at ease. And I'm beginning to suspect why, when Yumei's smile confirms what I'm thinking: Dr. Vogt has left.

She immediately gets up and walks over to two hard-looking Chinese men in blue. She's explaining things to them. Things they don't seem happy to hear. Before I can get a sense of what they're planning, a whistle goes up and the prisoners move toward the center of the dusty rec area.

They form a haphazard circle, and I make my way to the outskirts, wondering what's going on. As I move closer, two men in blue scrubs are pushed into the center. An older, heavyset man who looks like he was built for life behind a desk, and a skinny guy with a shaved head and a lot of ink that looks to be of the white-power variety.

A chant goes up from the crowd.

"Fight. Fight. Fight!"

The two men look terrified to be at the center of this. They're both searching for someone to help them, to tell them this is some kind of joke. I follow their gaze and find a couple of owls standing along the top of the wall, looking down.

Watching.

Shit.

They're not going to stop it.

Someone yells, "You know how this works!"

Of the two men, the younger man seems to accept his fate. He runs at the heavyset man and throws himself into the man's gut. They tumble to the ground in a tangle of limbs, and it's hard to see what's happening because there are people crowded in front of me, and that old part of me that relishes the taste of blood and mayhem wants to get closer. But the newer parts of me, the ones that believe in redemption, want to turn and run.

Whatever happens, it doesn't take long. The younger man gets up, blood flowing from a gash on his forehead. The heavier man is still moving, holding his face, blood seeping through his fingers. They move away from each other, the fight over. So this isn't a to-the-death kind of thing.

Two more men in blue take their place. Both of them look like they have a military or fighting background, from the precision in their stances. They start to circle each other, but they seem to relish the opportunity a little more. They go careful, testing distances, feeling each other out.

"A way to pass the time," a voice behind me says.

I turn to find a tall, beautiful man with wavy dark hair and a goatee. He's wearing a pink jumpsuit with the arms ripped off.

"Is it, now?"

He nods. "I'm Domingo. You are new here. It is not often we get new faces."

The two men continue moving carefully, almost like they're running out a clock. A boo goes up from the audience.

"Just so you're aware," Domingo says, "if you ever need anything, I'm your man."

"Every prison has a guy, and I guess you're the guy," I say.

He smiles. "I'm the guy."

"Can you get me a jet pack so I can fly out of here?"

"I can't get you anything that won't fit inside an ass," he says. "The guards are strip-searched on their way in. I have a few that'll work with me, but it's hard to move contraband."

"How many guards are there per shift?"

"Twenty. That's to thirty-two inmates. New shift comes in every five days."

Those are important numbers to know; I file them away.

The two men finally engage, and the fight doesn't last long. It looks more like friendly sparring than it does a blood sport, and the enthusiasm of the crowd beings to dim.

"Well, thanks, but I know nothing in life is free, and I'm currently a little light on cash . . ."

Domingo smiles. "I'll accept the odd favor, but I mostly provide my services free of charge."

"Bullshit."

"I am here because I opposed the Brazilian president, a man named Azevedo . . ." he starts.

"I know who Azevedo is," I tell him. "Partido Liberal. Always thought it was funny that the most conservative party in the country called itself the Liberal Party."

Domingo nods. "Azevedo built this place. It was already a restricted area because of the snakes. Now he makes a mint off it. But he did promise the people he would offer more housing options."

"Should you even be talking about this?" I ask. "What about all the microphones?"

He smiles. "Out here, all the wind and the noise? One of the only safe places to speak."

"What about—"

Before I can finish, something knocks me hard from behind, throwing me forward through the crowd. I manage to get my hands up to stop from smashing my face on the ground, but I'm pretty sure I sprain both wrists in the process.

I look up to find one of the Chinese men that Yumei was speaking with. There's a crunch behind me, and I turn to find the other man. I slowly get to my feet and there's a yell from the crowd, "Blues only!"

A door opens across the yard, and an owl comes out. There are two more owls in the yard. I'd say they were talking to one another but since I can't see their faces, it's not like I can be sure. After a moment, the three of them turn around and go inside.

It's just the inmates now.

Payback for Godfrey.

My stomach falls, watching them go, and I just barely catch one of the men throw a cheap no-look kick at my leg. I barely get my shin up in time to check it, but then the other man comes at me and drives his fist into my gut, shifting and bruising things inside me.

The crowd proceeds to cheer.

I guess the pink jumpsuit only offers me so much protection.

As I stumble, the man who struck me follows, so I get on my toes and hop back to create space. I snap out a jab, to slow his momentum, then use that as an opportunity to slip away. Now that I've got some space and can move around, I feel a little better.

That's short-lived. Yumei throws herself into my midsection, knocking me against the ground, and I crack my head. I'm suddenly woozy, and she's holding on for dear life, so I bring my fist down hard on her spine. She screams and arches her back, as the other two men take advantage of my distraction and lay into me.

From there it's a flurry of pain, until a voice yells, "Stop!"

I look up and find Quraishi.

He's walked to the center of the ring, and everyone has stopped. Even Yumei. The only sound is the rustling of the wind and the heavy labor of my breath. Every single person around us takes a few steps back, giving him a wider berth. The fear is palpable, like Death himself just stepped into the circle.

The two Chinese men immediately put up their hands and

back away, heads bowed, muttering apologies. Yumei gets up, too, and she looks at him before baring her teeth and following.

Quraishi watches them disappear to the other side of the yard as I move myself into a sitting position. My body is knotted together with pain. It's mostly centered in my ego. I'm tired. My body is still processing whatever drugs they put into me. I'm not at my best. That's why they got me on the ground.

At my peak that never would have happened.

The rest of the crowd goes back to what they were doing before the festivities started.

"May I sit?"

Quraishi has a book clasped in front of him. I look at him for a moment, consider it. He nods and begins to walk away, but I remember what Mark would say: that none of us are perfect.

"Sure," I tell him.

He turns back and sits on the ground next to me, crossing his legs like a schoolchild. He places the book in front of him. *Haroun and the Sea of Stories* by Salman Rushdie.

"That's an interesting choice," I tell him.

"The library is small, and there aren't many options," he says. "But this is very good. I can lend it to you when I'm done."

I tug at my uniform. "Thought we weren't supposed to be harmed."

"Only so much," he says. "The doctor is a . . . calming presence. He never leaves for more than a day at a time. When he is gone, the rules change. It is unlikely they would have killed you. But they would have done their best to hurt you."

"Lovely." I go to thank him, and the words get stuck. He notices this and smiles.

"You are welcome," he says, with a kindness and warmth that make me feel ashamed.

And then I remember who this man is.

"I make you uncomfortable," he says.

"Do you blame me?"

"No," he says. "I do not."

We sit in silence for a little while. I watch Yumei with her two friends. They break off from her and go inside. I suspect I will be seeing them again soon. Yumei heads over to a heavy bag installed into the side wall and throws a flurry of punches at it. They're sloppy, but they're determined. She glances over every few minutes to make sure I'm looking.

"I appreciate your reticence to trust me," Quraishi says. "I do not know why you are here. But it is clear to see that there is something special about you. Something that the doctor or someone else wants. I would offer you my assistance. Even my friendship."

"Why?" I ask.

"Because I see the same sadness in your eyes that I feel in mine."

Giving help.

Getting help.

What has that ever gotten me?

A lot of people dead.

Chea.

Godfrey.

Maybe my entire home group.

Lucia?

No. No one else gets hurt. I do this alone.

"I didn't ask for your help," I tell Quraishi, as I climb to my feet. "And I don't need it. We're nothing alike. And I'm better off alone."

Mark's voice rings in my head in response.

No, you're not.

But I block it out.

MARK

London
Now

A door creaks open, and an older woman comes shuffling out of an apartment down the hall. She's heading away from us, toward the elevator, but manages to catch sight of me and Booker, sitting on the floor of the hallway, against the door of the apartment we're waiting to get inside. Her gaze lingers on Booker.

I wave my hand at her. "Good afternoon, ma'am. Just waiting for our friend. Should be here any minute."

She seems to raise an eyebrow at that, but then disappears into the elevator.

"She's definitely calling the cops," Booker says, as he turns his wooden rosary beads over in his hands. "Black man sitting in the hallway."

"Only one of us is Black," I say. "Maybe it cancels out?"

He smacks me on the arm and laughs from deep within his chest. "Asshole."

And then we go back to waiting.

I stretch my shoulders and twist my neck, still stiff from the flight. I would have treated us to first class, but we booked so close to departure we had to settle for two economy seats. Felt like seven hours crammed in a sardine can.

Booker sighs deeply, fidgeting beside me, fingering the beads of the rosary. He didn't sleep, either. We each got a pair of those shitty free headphones from the flight attendant and tried to find a movie to watch together, but we couldn't agree, so I went with *Casablanca*—I'll never not watch *Casablanca* if it's an option—and Booker went for one of the Marvel movies. I don't know which one. It had Captain America in it, but a lot of them do.

"Hey, man, you good?" I ask.

"Tired," Booker says. "How much longer?"

"I'd call him if I felt safe doing it." I look down at my watch. We've been here two hours now. "Wish he'd show up."

"She's going to be okay," Booker says. "You know that, right? She got us a message, and anyway, she's tough as shit. I'd rather tussle with you than with her."

"She asked for help. I don't want to let her down."

"You can't open the cocoon for her," Booker says.

"The hell is that supposed to mean?"

Booker puts his hands up in front of him, like he's trying to outline a shape, the rosary dangling in the air. "Thing about a cocoon is, it's hard for the butterfly to get out of, right? But it's part of the process. If you open the cocoon for the butterfly, its wings won't be strong enough to fly. It's got to do that part on its own."

"That's a good one," I tell him. "I'm stealing that from you.

But it doesn't apply. We're not going to leave her . . . wherever she is."

"Not what I was saying. I just mean that . . ."

The elevator dings, and off steps Gaius. He's wearing expensive selvedge-denim jeans, along with a white tank top adorned with flamingos, and a pair of gold headphones over his ears. He sees me and Booker and shakes his head. "I don't recall giving you my new address, bruv."

"Yeah, but I'm good at what I do," I tell him. "You should invite us in before the cops get here." I point toward the door at the end of the hall that the old lady came out of. "That one over there gave us the stink eye."

Gaius nods. "Yeah, she's racist as shit. Let's get inside."

We stand and he brushes past us, then exchanges a fist bump with Booker.

"Least one of you is white, or else the fuzz would definitely be here by now . . ." Gaius mutters, under his breath.

"See?" I tell Booker.

Booker just rolls his eyes.

The new place is not too different from his old one, which he gave up most likely because of the time I stormed in, threatened him, and forced him to give me some information I needed. Granted, the information he fed me was bad, which I didn't know at the time, and I don't blame him for that, because I would have done the same in his shoes.

Since then he's become something of an ally. I can say that because the false identity he set up for me seems to be working so far.

Gaius leads us into the living room, which holds a massively expensive television, a ton of gaming consoles, and laptops carefully placed around the room. It's a cluttered but cozy space. I appreciate that he lives below the radar. The man has to be worth a few hundred million, easily—he's the webmaster of the Amber Road, and he gets a cut of every drug that's sold, every contract taken on someone's life. All completely anonymized, so he doesn't have to spend a lot of time looking over his shoulder. I'd call it a good business model, but *good* doesn't seem like the right word in this case.

"Gaius, Booker; Booker, Gaius," I say, pointing between the two of them, before I plop down onto the couch. I take off my goofy glasses and toss them on the coffee table.

"Make yourself at home," Gaius says, then nods to the eyepiece. "Those things working out for you okay?"

"So far so good. I'm alive."

Booker folds down on the couch next to me and immediately falls into the arm of it, trying to get comfortable. I won't be shocked if he's snoring within the next three minutes.

Gaius sits in a wingback chair across from us. "So, you show up on my doorstep, unannounced, and I suspect it ain't for a social visit. Should I be worried?"

"Not yet," I tell him. "I need information."

He nods and sighs. "Anyone need a drink?"

Booker is leaning his head against his arm, fighting a losing battle against gravity. "Anything that's going to wake me up."

Gauis goes to the kitchen and comes back with two aluminum cans with Chinese writing down the sides. "Those got enough caffeine in 'em you shouldn't have more than one in a day. But it looks like you could both use it."

I crack it open and take a sip—it tastes like candy, but in a not-unpleasant way. Booker takes his can and guzzles half of it in one go. Gaius sits again and picks up a laptop, cradling it on his thighs, and says, "What are we doing?"

I explain to him what I need—phone records from a pizza place, yesterday, to determine the point of origin of a call—and leave it at that. He doesn't need more details. He shakes his head and laughs. "Came all the way here for that?"

"There are other factors at play here, and people I'm trying to keep safe," I tell him.

"How do I know when I find the right number?"

"Not sure," I say. "Let's start with anything that looks strange."

I recite the address for the pizza place. After a few moments, Booker is snoring. Guess that caffeine needs time to kick in. I'm about to ask how long this might take when Gaius nods. "Obviously they take a lot of phone calls," he says, "but there's one right here that came in from Brazil. Just ran it back, and that's where the phone is registered. Brazil. Now hold on . . ."

Gaius squints at the screen. "Huh."

"What's 'huh'?" I ask.

"Call was made about twenty miles off the coast. Just . . . wait." Gaius leans forward and squints at the screen. "Nah, that can't be right. Il-ha da Quei-mada Grande," he says, fumbling over the syllables. Then his eyes go wide. "Shit."

He turns the laptop around to show me an aerial photo of an island with rocky shores and green vegetation around the center. "The call came from a place called Snake Island. Full of poisonous snakes. It's not even open to the public."

I poke Booker and he jerks awake, immediately bringing his fists up to his chin like he's getting into fighting stance. "The fuck?" he asks.

I point to Gaius. "Astrid is on a restricted island off the coast of Brazil that's covered in poisonous snakes."

"Who's Astrid?" Gaius asks.

"Immaterial to your role in this," I tell him, and I turn to Booker. "What do you make of that?"

Booker shakes his head and says, "Yeah, man, that's a bit of a conundrum right there."

"Maybe not," I say. "Azevedo is still the president of Brazil, right? Corrupt as the day is long. And if I were a corrupt president looking to line my pockets, and I happened to have an island that was otherwise restricted and overall hostile . . ."

Booker snaps his fingers. "Black site."

"Bingo," I tell him. "We know Astrid is being held. We know she's being kept alive. It's the only thing that makes sense given the circumstances. It could be something else, but, you know, hoofbeats and horses."

"What about horses?" Gaius asks.

"When you hear hoofbeats," I tell him, "you think horses, not zebras."

"So like Occam's razor," he says.

"Same thing." I sit back and put my hands behind my head. The caffeine is taking its time showing up. We've got a working theory, but we need intel. "Book, you got any contacts in Brazil?"

"I know some people, yeah," he says. "You?"

"Nothing," I tell him. "Gaius, is there any way . . ."

Gaius is typing furiously on his laptop. "I mean, you'd think a project like that would leave a trail, but the problem is they probably tried to cover their tracks, and I wouldn't even know what to look for. Needle in a haystack, like. Give me a few days, maybe . . ."

"Not sure if we have a few days," I tell him.

"She's stayed alive for a month," Booker says.

"And maybe getting in contact with us put her in peril, or she's desperate." I press my hands into my face, trying to rub the exhaustion away. "I guess we go down there and see what we can find."

Booker nods and says, "As long as we're here, I've got a friend in town I can check in with. He's got some good international contacts. Can't hurt, right?"

"Right," I say. "Want me to come?"

"Nah," he says. "Better if I handle solo. Why don't you post up someplace and I'll see if I can raise him."

"Sure thing," I say. Then I pull a wad of cash out of my pocket, count off two grand, and toss it on the table in front of Gaius. "That about cover ten minutes' worth of work?" I ask.

Gaius nods. "It does. And next time, call first?"

I'm on my third espresso and my heart feels like it's going to rocket out of my chest and splatter on the wall of this cute little café.

At least I'm awake now.

I hope this doesn't take long—there are a couple of flights leaving later tonight that'll get us to where we need to be, and most of them include first-class seats. The nice kind that convert into a bed, and it's a twelve-hour flight, which means we can catch up on sleep on the way down.

My phone buzzes. A text from Booker: Almost there.

I stash my phone and watch the street. Apparently Booker's friend can help us, and the two of them are coming here so we can come up with a game plan.

This is fantastic news.

Until it's not.

Because I catch sight of Booker crossing the street with a man I know.

Jean Lavigne.

Last time I was in London I stopped into the local AA chapter. I was struggling. Unfortunately, it coincided with my identity as the Pale Horse being made public, and it turned out a whole bunch of people in that meeting did not like me. A few seemed willing to break their sobriety if it meant collecting my scalp.

Most especially Lavigne, a French assassin whose ear I took off with a sniper rifle to protect an Algerian Islamic militant he had wanted to kill, but the United States had wanted to question. I got the green light to kill Lavigne, but chose to let him live and slow him down.

He did not see it as an act of generosity.

They enter the café and Lavigne sees me and stops cold. He and Booker exchange words. Booker rolls his eyes, like, *of course.* Booker heads to the counter, presumably to order for them, and Lavigne sits across from me. His face is blank, but his shoulders are tensed, like he might spring across the table at me.

Before I can speak Booker puts a cup of espresso down in front of Lavigne and says, "Gonna give you two a moment to sort things out, then."

He heads toward the back of the café, out of earshot. I twist in my chair, to make sure there's no one else close by, and turn back to Lavigne, trying my best not to stare at the mottle of skin over his left ear.

My handiwork.

His burden.

"So," I tell him, "this is awkward."

Lavigne takes a short sip of his espresso, then places the tiny mug back down with a *clink*. "I told him we have a history, but did not offer specifics."

"How do you two know each other?" I ask.

Lavigne shrugs. "Around. Booker tells me that a fellow is in need of help."

"Look, I owe you an amends. And I wasn't exactly prepared to make it right now, but I'd like to try, if you would be open to it."

His eyes widen, and I wonder if he's surprised that I'm so willing to gloss over him trying to kill me the last time I saw him, or if it's just the audacity of the ask. I choose to believe the former.

He doesn't respond, so I launch into it.

"I'll spare you the speech about how the job is the job," I tell him. "You understand as well as I do how it works. I don't wish to excuse my actions, because I can't. I can only explain them. I know you were after Zain Hassan. I know the mission was somewhat personal for you. My organization needed him alive for questioning. They knew you planned to kill him and they gave me the order to execute you. I thought the kinder thing to do would be to slow you down, which is why I took your ear. Even saying it now, I know how ridiculous that sounds. Maybe there was a better way to handle that situation, but I was never taught to use my words. I can't undo it and I am truly sorry for what I did to you."

Lavigne nods slowly, taking another sip of the espresso, and looks around the café.

"You sat there," he says finally. "You listened to me bare my soul about the daily pain this brings me. That I cannot look in the mirror without being reminded of the things I used to do. You sat there and you listened and you said nothing."

"In fairness," I say, "you did almost immediately try to kill me when you found out I used to be the Pale Horse. In that moment I convinced myself I was protecting you, but the truth is, I was protecting myself. I could have owned up to it in that moment, and I should have."

He puts his hands on the table and sighs. "I have information that will be useful. I will help you find your friend."

The directness knocks me off balance. "Just like that."

"I will come with you," he says. "I will help you bring her home. She is a fellow, and we are all bound by the program."

I laugh a little. "Man, I thought that was going to be a lot harder . . ."

"When we return, when the job is done, you will give me your ear," he says.

"Oh."

Again, knocked off balance.

"You expect me to just carve my ear off and hand it to you?" I ask.

"Yes," he says. "Or I can do it. Perhaps this is not in the spirit of the program, but I will pay you the same kindness you paid me. You will give me your ear, and we will be even. You will know what it is like to live with the constant reminder of your mistakes."

I want to tell him that I live with the reminder every day. What he sees in that scarred patch of flesh on the side of his head, I see in my eyes in the mirror. But I also understand that most times I'm the only one who sees that, while he has to deal with the stares of people around him.

And this is for Astrid.

I can live with one ear.

"Deal," I tell him.

"Thank you," he says.

We shake. I expect his hand to envelop mine, to crush it as a sign of dominance, but instead his grip is soft and friendly.

Then he puts up his hand and waves at Booker, who comes to the table and sets down his own mug and saucer.

"Glad to see you two playing nice," he says.

"Right," I tell him, and Lavigne gives me a little smile and a wink.

"I have been to the island where they are keeping your friend," Lavigne says. "Six months ago. A man I had crossed paths with once is being held there. Fahad Quraishi."

Booker's face drops. "You danced with the Shiqq?"

Holy shit.

People used to say I was the most dangerous man in the world.

The Shiqq scares *me*.

"My government had some questions to ask him," he says. "I went to ask them, as a favor. The DGSE brokered the deal. I was to be taken there blindfolded, to preserve the secrecy of the location."

"How do you know for sure where it was?" I ask.

"Another favor," he says, craning his neck and pulling aside the collar of his shirt, revealing a tiny scar. "The DGSE implanted a tracker in my neck. We had every assurance that I would be returned safely, but they wanted to verify the location."

"Hell of a favor," I tell him.

"Some of us owe big debts, and would do anything to clear them."

Booker has no idea how pointed those words are.

"I spoke to a contact," Lavigne says. "Based on the intelligence they have since collected, I am to understand that the prison receives regular shipments by helicopter, from a port in Guarujá. I believe we could commandeer one of those transports, posing as guards."

"This might get messy," Booker says. "Mark and I live in acceptance of the things we might need to sacrifice. We can't ask you to do the same."

Lavigne smiles, holding my eyes with his. "It is for a fellow."

"Okay," I tell them, whipping out my phone. "I guess I'm booking three tickets. We'll fly into São Paulo and make our way there. You have clean info to travel on, I imagine?"

Lavigne goes to the counter and comes back with a napkin and a pen, and jots down the details I need.

I should be thankful for this. I really should be. But I'm not.

Because already, the skin on my ear is tingling.

IV

Everything becomes a little different as soon as it is spoken out loud.

—HERMANN HESSE

ASTRID

Prospect Park, Brooklyn
Seven Years Ago

Chea trots a few paces ahead of me as we make our way around the lake. The sun is just cresting the horizon, but the park is already crowded with bikers and walkers and runners. That's summertime in Brooklyn. The entire borough turns into a carnival, celebrating the good weather.

I pump my legs a little and pull up alongside her. "You don't have to go so hard. This is just the warm-up."

"I like to run," she says, barely out of breath, her ponytail bobbing behind her.

The way she says it, I can understand.

We circle the park twice, the sun now higher and the two of us soaked through our workout clothes. We wander until we find an empty patch of grass. I pull off my backpack and we take out bottles of water and sip on them as we do a little yoga, to stretch out and loosen up.

And then we train.

It's been a year now, and she's already more filled out. She doesn't stand with a perpetual slouch. There's still a blankness in her eyes, but that's something that I can't do much about. Only time can fix that, and even then, the odds aren't fantastic.

"We're going to work defense today," I tell her. "You're short, and you don't weigh a lot. But you're fast. You need to train your response time. You start by learning how to absorb a blow. One of the hardest things about fighting is knowing how to take a hit and keep your brain working. Most people just go blank and panic. So get your guard up and I'm going to throw slow punches and kicks. You're not going to return, you're just going to focus on blocking. Understood?"

"Yes," Chea says, and she puts her hands up, knuckles tucked under her cheekbones.

"A little higher," I tell her. "It'll better protect your head, because I'm taller and can just punch over your guard. And it'll be easier on you when I start teaching you how to throw elbows."

Chea nods and lifts her arms. She looks more like a praying mantis than a boxer. I move toward her and throw a jab. She meets it with her hand, but I'm still able to push through.

"A little more force," I tell her. "Give me some resistance. Like we're playing patty-cake."

"I don't know . . . patty-cake?"

Another fissure opens in my heart, to join all the others she's put there, and I mourn the childhood she never had.

"Okay," I tell her. "Let's play patty-cake."

I walk her through it. We go slow at first, until we pick up speed. She seems to enjoy the rhyme of it, and she gets the rhythm quickly.

As we do this, she betrays the slightest hint of a smile, so fast that maybe it was a twitch of her lip. But I choose to take it as a smile.

"Okay," I tell her. "Let's take a break."

"But I'm ready."

"Slow is smooth and smooth is fast," I tell her. "Let the lessons sink in. We're not going anywhere."

Chea sits against the tree and looks out at the park. We linger in the silence for a bit, sipping our water. Sometimes we have to linger in the silence because I don't know what to say to this girl. I don't even know what I am to her.

The Agency set her up with paperwork so I could enroll her in school. But I didn't want to rush her on that. Figured it was best to let her acclimate to her new life before throwing her into the crucible of the New York City public school system. As afraid as I am to let her out of my sight, it'll do her good to be around other kids.

She already has a good grasp of English, so in the meantime I've been encouraging her to read a lot. She's been devouring books like they're oxygen. She likes fantasy novels. I could never get into them—the first word I can't pronounce, my brain sputters and sparks. But I understand her desire to read about far-off, fantastical lands, where magic is a thing and the heroes usually win. It's a hell of a lot better than this.

"Astrid . . ." she says.

"Yeah?"

"Why are you teaching me to fight?"

"Because . . ." I start, not having a great answer. "Because I'm not always going to be around to protect you."

"Is it because you want me to be like you?"

"I'm not . . ." But I trail off, not sure what she means by that.

"I found things. Underneath the floorboards in your bedroom."

That stops me cold.

It was only a matter of time. She's a kid, and kids are curious. We never had a direct conversation about what I was doing when our paths crossed, but I'm sure she figured it out, piecing the story together. I haven't been working as much, because I want to be around for her. But I also need to support us, and that means taking the occasional Agency gig, or patching up someone with a gunshot or stab wound who doesn't want to answer questions in a hospital.

"You kill people," Chea says.

"I fix them sometimes, too." My voice feels small when I say this, like it's a poor excuse for my life choices.

"But that's your job," she says, growing confident. "You're an assassin. I've seen movies."

"Chea, it's not like that . . ."

"I want to be like you," she says.

She fixes me with a hard stare when she says this. In that moment the scared little girl vanishes and I see something built of sterner stuff.

"You don't want to be like me," I tell her. "It's a lonely life.

It's dangerous. Always looking over my shoulder. Hell, taking you in might have been a mista—"

The word catches on my teeth, but I don't need to finish it. Chea's eyes widen, for an instant, and then she leans against the tree, staring up into the foliage. Her face tenses. She's fighting back tears.

"I didn't mean it like that," I tell her. "I'm glad you're here. I just don't ever want to put you in any kind of danger."

"Why are you training me then?"

"Because . . ." I start, searching for the words. "Because the world is a hard place."

We sit under the tree and sip on our waters, looking out over the roadway—the bikers and the runners passing us by, oblivious to the crushing weight of this conversation. What I said was the truth, but it wasn't the whole truth.

I know why I do this job. It's an outlet for the anger that lives in my chest like a wild animal, and sometimes that animal needs to claw its way out. What I do, I can say it makes the world a better place, but really, I just like hurting men, and this job, it's mostly men I have to hurt.

Maybe she deserves a taste of that, too.

"Are you leaving anytime soon?" she asks, her voice suddenly cold. Changing the subject.

"No," I tell her. "Things are quiet."

Chea struggles when I'm away. It's never more than a few days but she still wakes up screaming with nightmares, and on the nights I'm not there to comfort her, I dread to think of what that looks like, her all alone in the apartment.

But I still have to work.

I expected to do that work and live alone.

"Can we go to the library today?" she asks.

"Already? It's been three days? You got four books."

She shrugs, offering me a little smirk.

"I'm proud of you," I tell her.

She beams when I say this.

"I'm sorry, about asking," Chea says. "I just want to be strong like you."

"You are strong like me. Look at where you ended up." I gesture around the park. "Did you ever think it could be like this?"

"No," she says. "Not even in my dreams."

"I promise you, this lifestyle is nothing like the movies. It's not putting on fancy dresses and sneaking around. It's hard, and it's scary, and it's lonely."

Chea looks at me, and for the first time, offers me an actual smile. Eye contact and everything. And she says the most brutal thing she could possibly say in this moment.

"But we have each other."

That nearly breaks me in two.

Maybe this is what she deserves. An outlet. A way to take those broken things inside her and knit them back together.

Sometimes the best way to do that is to break something else.

A harsh whistle erupts, shattering my thoughts. I look up at the roadway, where a man on a bike is slowly drifting past, ogling the both of us, but paying special attention to Chea.

The sight of him leering at her sets something off inside me, and I test the weight of my water bottle. It's still half-full.

"She's underage, you asshole," I yell.

And then I wing the water bottle at his head. It sails true, smacking him clear in the forehead and knocking him off his bike. He goes down hard, yelling, then gets tangled in his bike as he's trying to get up.

Chea laughs. So do I.

"We should get the hell out of here," I say.

"Good plan," she says.

And we resume our jog, back toward my apartment.

"If we're going to do this," I tell her, "you have to listen to everything I say. No matter what."

She nods. "I will." Then she turns and throws herself into my midsection, stopping us in our tracks, her small body clinging to me. "Thank you, Astrid."

I kiss her on the top of her head. "You got it, kiddo."

We resume our run, but now it feels like we're running toward something, rather than away from it.

ASTRID

The Tenth Circle
Now

S he is not pleased . . ."
  Words drifting through the ether upon waking.

She is not pleased.

She?

Dr. Vogt said it to someone toward the end of our latest
session.

That's something. That's more than I've had thus far.

The person holding me here is a woman.

In this moment of fuzzy-brained awakening it doesn't do
much to narrow the list. I can say with some level of confidence that I haven't had direct issues with women very often in
my career, Yumei aside, and she can't be the one behind this.

She.

Someone's wife? Their daughter?

I can work with that.

I consider a shower—it usually gives me an opportunity to clear the drug-induced haze from my head after the sessions— but before I can do that, a scream slices through the silence of the prison. On instinct I leap off the cot and yank the door open, trying to locate the source of it.

Across the way is an older Hispanic man in a blue jumpsuit with bushy black hair, lying in a fetal position on the floor, two owls standing over him like they're waiting for directions. The man's head jerks a few times and then he vomits a long stream of dark liquid across the floor. It looks like blood. Then he screams again.

The owls grab him under his arms, his body rag-doll limp, and they drag him away, the concrete floor still streaked with the thick, sticky liquid, and the horrible stench drifting toward me. I breathe through my mouth and follow. I'm not sure what else to do. There's no one around; I have no idea what time it is. And if everyone is out in the yard, that's great, but I'm not in the mood for fight club.

The owls drag the man down a hallway, before tossing him into a room and closing the door. His screams are muffled as the door closes. They turn to look at me and their gaze feels like a spotlight, prickling my skin.

The two of them advance and I set myself, head still swimming, but ready in case this becomes a thing, when a voice behind me says, "Astrid."

I turn to find Dr. Vogt.

The owls freeze. Caught by daddy. The doctor says, "I am so glad you're up. Would you please join me?" He looks at the owls and says, "Você pode ficar no corredor."

You can stay in the hallway.

They hesitate, then turn and walk away. Dr. Vogt gestures toward his office, welcoming me inside, and shuts the door. "Please, sit," he says, as he walks around his desk, falling heavily into his seat. He has bags under his eyes, and his face has a day or two of stubble growth.

I sit and wave behind me. "Pretty bold. Who's to say I'm not going to snap your neck?"

"Please, Astrid. You know you can't kill me."

I do my best not to betray any emotion at that, but it's hard. Does he know about Assassins Anonymous? That would be . . . not good. It's one of the challenges of being in the program. You don't want to kill anyone anymore, but it's not always good when people know you won't kill.

Sometimes the aura of your past life is the only shield you've got. It saved Mark's ass last year, even though he ultimately decided that he didn't want to dip back into the Pale Horse persona—it felt the same as killing to him, using the power granted to him by the name. A rush is a rush.

But in here, right now, I need all the armor I can get.

So I do the only thing I can think to do—I leap up onto the desk, grab a pen, and hold it to his neck. I try to hide the fact that I'm still woozy from the drugs working their way out of my system, but I think he sees it in my eyes.

I get close to his ear and ask, "How do you know I won't kill you?"

He smiles and leans into the pen. It indents his skin.

"You were not given a proper orientation when you arrived," he says, then softly pats his chest. "I've been so busy, I apologize. I didn't explain the Medusa Protocol to you."

I let off the pressure on the pen a little.

"The hell is that?"

"Please sit," he says.

The confidence in his voice is enough to get me to comply.

He pats his chest again, over his heart. "I have a pacemaker, and in this pacemaker is what's called a dead man's switch. I'm sure you understand what that is?"

"A switch that activates if your heart stops."

He nods, smiling. "Correct. Astrid . . ." He leans forward, with a let-me-level-with-you vibe. "You must understand. This institution houses some of the most dangerous people on the planet. If we were to lose control of the population, it would be immensely dangerous. All of you out there, running around unchecked. So if I am killed, the protocol activates, and every security measure"—he blows and makes a little poof with his hands—"ceases to be. Every door opens. Every electrical circuit fried. You wouldn't even be able to call for help. And there are devices, under the prison, designed to create vibrations that will attract the snakes."

"Why not just blow the place up?"

He shakes his head. "Someone would notice that, on satellite imagery or some such, and it's important that, even in the event of an emergency, this place remain a secret. So you see, I am quite safe within these walls."

"I guess we better just hope you don't get hit by a bus when you're off campus."

He laughs. "The switch only works when I'm on the island. For what it's worth, the guards have access to a fail-safe that would trigger the protocol as well, so, ultimately hurting me or trying to escape won't result in anything good, for anyone."

"And the guards are just down to die for the cause?"

"They are paid very well. And they all signed a waiver."

We sit in silence for a little, Vogt with that impish smile, so excited to explain this to me.

"That guy out there," I ask, "what happened to him?"

Vogt looks momentarily confused before nodding. "Ah. Diego Vilano," he says, pronouncing the name carefully, enunciating each syllable. "Head of a drug cartel in Mexico."

"He's in blue, so, expendable?"

"He is the subject of the project I am working on."

"How wonderfully vague. Should I call you Dr. Mengele, then?"

Vogt's face twists in disgust. "Please. Mengele was a monster, and I find it both unfair and presumptuous to compare me to a Nazi just because of my origins." He raises his hand and waves it around. "Diego Vilano slaughtered hundreds of people."

"So he's a lab rat," I tell him. "You're torturing him."

"If the drug I'm testing on him is effective—which I grant you, thus far it is not—it would save countless lives. Who is Diego Vilano compared to the future of humanity?"

"He's a person."

"He is a person who has sinned deeply, beyond recompense. And may his life, or his death, contribute something positive to the world."

"So how long before you start pumping me with experimental drugs? Does my captor have to sign off on that? Whoever *she* is?"

Dr. Vogt gently raises and then drops his shoulders. "She?"

"You said, 'She is not pleased,'" I tell him.

He smiles. "Interesting. *Very* interesting. So you can hear what I am saying, despite the state that you are in?" He pulls a notepad from across the desk and scribbles on it, mumbling to himself. "That should not be the case with the compounds I am using, but perhaps I have the dosage wrong. How much exactly do you weigh?" Then he waves his hand. "Nonsense, you wouldn't know considering the diet we've had you on . . ."

"Hey, Doc, maybe get excited about this later. Tell me who she is."

"You understand I am not at liberty to divulge that. We have had this conversation, Astrid." The way he says it is like a disappointed parent.

"Then just tell me what she's after," I say. "If she wants to torture me, fine, tell me that. But there's a halfway decent chance that whatever she wants I'll be happy to part with."

"I do not believe this to be true," he says.

"How can you know that?" I ask.

"Based on the things I have learned . . ." He sits back in his seat and breathes deeply, like he's tired. "Surely you understand what it is I'm doing. I'm trying to extract certain memories from you. It does no harm to tell you that I am using a combination of drugs and hypnosis to do so. It is my primary field of research. It is why I don't go in for, as you so delightfully put it, fingernail peeling. It simply doesn't work. The human psyche cannot be forced. It must be finessed. Weakened first." He drifts for a moment, before looking back at me. "I hope to turn this facility into the foremost institution for memory retrieval."

"That's some supervillain shit," I tell him.

"Ah, but think about it," he says. "What is the most valuable thing in the world? It's not real estate. It's *information*. And all these prisons all over the world, trying to extract information from people who don't want to give it up, all those government officials, one day they will just come knocking at my door, with the assurance that the things I give them will be true. How many lives we'll be able to save. Torture is a barbaric, useless thing. I will offer a path that is not only kind, but more effective."

"So you're developing some kind of truth serum? Is that what you're giving to me?"

Vogt snaps his fingers. "Exactly. Scopolamine, midazolam, sodium thiopental, amobarbital . . . there is no *true* truth serum with predictable and consistent results. I aim to develop a compound that actually works. In the meantime, my work is in a more experimental phase. I am testing a new compound on Diego, which unfortunately, does not seem to be sitting well with him. What I'm using on you is slightly more tested. Much safer, though not producing the effect I'm seeking."

"So you can tell me that much. Not privileged."

He nods. "Now, if you knew specifically what I was looking for, I suspect it might be possible for you to resist the retrieval of that particular memory. To put a wall around it. And I know it's information you would never give freely. So, we must continue the work. And I am sorry to say, Astrid, that my current methods are not working as intended. We may have to move on to more invasive techniques."

The air feels suddenly sucked out of the room, and I have to remind myself to breathe. "Such as?"

"Deep brain stimulation," he says. "I would insert probes into your skull and use electrical impulses to fire your memory centers."

"You're going to drill into my brain?"

"It is a last resort, and one I do not relish," he says. "I am not even sure if it would be effective. Your benefactor is encouraging me to use it, and is quite insistent about achieving results sooner rather than later. She is on a clock, it seems. So I am telling you this as someone who cares about your well-being: open yourself to the process."

"You're drugging me and interrogating me, and you care about my well-being? You want me to be more open?"

Vogt frowns. "I am a doctor, Astrid. It is not my desire to actively hurt anyone. I do not want to hurt Diego Vilano. I want to save lives. There is a cost to that. And I can tell you for sure that if we have to take the brain-stimulation route, I cannot ensure your safety."

"So that's it, then?" I ask. "Let you dig into my brain and scramble it for reasons you won't tell me, and if I don't relax and keep resisting you'll just do worse."

"Pretty much, yes."

I want more than anything to dive across the desk and rip open his carotid artery with my teeth, but I know that's going to get me—and a whole lot of other people—dead.

Because my actions have consequences.

Just ask Godfrey.

"Who picked the name?" I ask. "Medusa."

He shrugs. "I did."

"Why?"

"Seemed fitting, given the location."

"Do you know the story of Medusa?" I ask. When he blinks at me, like I'm boring him now, I tell him, "She was beautiful. And devoted to the goddess Athena. So beautiful she caught the eye of Poseidon, and when she wouldn't submit to him, he raped her on the steps of Athena's temple. But in the time-honored tradition of blaming the victim, Athena took her rage out on Medusa, taking away her beauty, turning her hair to snakes, making it so her gaze turned people to stone. Even then, she didn't want to hurt anyone, so she went and lived in solitude. Until Perseus, the son of Zeus, showed up one day and cut her head off, so he could make a name for himself. After her death, she was reduced to an object. Turned into a weapon."

Vogt nods. "I did not know that. Thank you for sharing that with me."

"I figured you didn't," I tell him, before leaving the office and closing the door.

I brush past the owl waiting outside. It must be mealtime; I can smell the food, but my stomach doesn't feel ready to bear it, so I head toward my cell, where I can safely be overwhelmed by the most terrible sense of dread at what it is they want from me.

Whatever it is must be very, very bad.

Right now, I am the weapon.

There's only one thing I know for sure: something in my head could be used to hurt someone, and I won't stand for that. I made a decision to stop hurting people, to stop killing people, because I realized it was doing nothing to fill the void in my soul. It was just making the void bigger.

I need to get the hell out of here.

MARK

São Paulo
Now

Lavigne and I watch Booker from across the street, as he huddles in the doorway of an apartment building marred with graffiti. I'm scanning the block, and Lavigne is doing the same. There's an old woman walking a dog, a little kid on a bike, and that's it. Doesn't look like anyone is watching us from the windows.

We're safe, I think. I hope.

I slept okay on the plane, and summer in the northern hemisphere means it's wintertime here, which translates to a pleasant 70 degrees under overcast skies. Small mercies.

I offer Lavigne the paper bag of pão de queijo, still warm from the bakery around the corner. He looks at it like it's filled with roaches, but then plucks one out and sticks it in his mouth. This was the thing I was most excited to try and I'm glad we had time. I've had Brazilian cheese bread before, but not in Brazil, which I figured would make a difference, and it does. Lactose intolerance be damned.

Lavigne finished, swallows, and says, "This changes nothing."

"Didn't think it would," I tell him. "Let me ask you something."

Lavigne doesn't respond.

"How'd you get the handle Noire?" I ask. "Because I'll tell you what, it's pretty dope. Nice and simple. The Pale Horse was a pretty cool name, too, but always felt like a bit of a mouthful."

Thirty seconds pass.

Then a minute.

"What do you think about this plan?" Lavigne finally asks, gesturing to the building.

Okay then. No small talk.

I crane my neck to peer at the top of the structure. Thirteen stories, currently occupied by squatters, like many of the buildings in the area. Doesn't exactly feel like the safest or the smartest plan, but it's the one we've got. I'm just hoping we can get out of here smoothly with what we need.

"Booker says he knows a guy," I tell him. "If he says it, I believe him. I just hope this guy isn't another one who wants to kill me."

"I only want your ear," Lavigne says.

"Yeah, we established that."

The man Booker is talking to disappears into the building. Booker turns to us and holds his hand up, telling us to wait. This is a process. That's fine.

We have to commandeer a helicopter and storm a black site prison twenty-something miles off the coast. We need weapons, and we couldn't exactly carry an arsenal onto the plane. It's nerve-racking enough to travel with fake passports.

This squat, apparently, is run by a weapons dealer.

But, a nice one.

Or so Booker says.

I offer the bag to Lavigne and he plucks out another piece of bread. "Let me ask you something else."

Lavigne sighs.

"Where do you think people like you and I are going to go, once we meet the end?"

Lavigne chews and swallows and doesn't say anything, for long enough that I wonder if he plans to ignore my every attempt to buddy up. Then he says, "We all must pay a price, eventually."

"Do you think what we're doing now—the program, the amends—will make any difference?" I ask. "Will it change the trajectory? Or are we headed due south, no matter what we do?"

"If there is a hell, then we've earned our spot there," Lavigne says. "But whatever punishment is handed to me, it will never compare to the ways in which I punish myself. Sometimes I think that is the price."

Yeah, seems like there's some wisdom to that.

I'm trying to think of something a little more cheery to discuss, when another man peers out of the cracked doorway, sees Booker, lights up, and pulls him into a big hug. He's a tall, thick guy with heavy stubble and an easy smile. Booker and the man exchange words and a laugh and then he waves us over.

"This is Enzo," Booker says, and Enzo steps forward, offering us his hand. When he takes mine, he grips it so hard I feel the bones in my hand shift, and then he pulls me into a hug. He does the same for Lavigne.

"Any friend of Booker . . ." he says, his voice booming, "is probably a piece of shit, but if your money is good, that's all that matters."

But then he gets a good look at my face and squints.

"You . . ."

"Yeah," I tell him. "I'm retired."

Enzo puffs his cheeks and exhales hard, then turns and smacks Booker on the chest. "I did not know you were bringing royalty to my doorstep."

"He's not as tough as he looks," Booker says, giving me a wink.

"It's true," I tell him, trying to hide my embarrassment. "Stories get bigger in the telling."

Enzo nods. "I suspect you have many stories to tell. My friends, come. It is a long walk to my office, but I believe I have what you need."

We step inside to the lobby. From the outside, the windows just looked dirty, but on the inside they're covered with curtains, to offer some degree of privacy, granting a cozy feel to the space. It's part bookstore, part art gallery, the concrete floor covered with overlapping scavenged carpets, easy chairs dotted around the space. A few of them are occupied by people, reading by candles in jars. There are lanterns, too, probably for when the sun sets.

It feels like a hip Williamsburg spot. I don't know what I was expecting, but it wasn't this.

Enzo sweeps his hand around the space, beaming with pride. "It is nice, no? I would love to tempt you with some cafezinho, but no one who ever comes to me for this type of business has time to linger."

"Seems like that would be the safest bet," Booker says.

We cross the space into a hallway, where the smell of grilled meat permeates the space. We pass a room with a makeshift kitchen, a battered charcoal grill set up next to a window to allow the smoke to billow out, tended to by an older man flipping large hunks of meat. A little boy rides his bicycle past us, down the hallway.

At the stairwell, Enzo takes the lead.

"What is this, exactly?" I ask.

"Sem-teto," Enzo says, as we slowly trudge up the stairs in a single file. "Brazil's roofless movement. Back in the 1990s, neighborhoods like this emptied out, leaving many of these buildings abandoned. Cost of living was getting too high, so many of the buildings were taken over by squatters."

"Can't the police come and clear you out?" Lavigne asks.

"They will stop you from getting in," Enzo says. "But once you are in, you have squatter's rights, and it becomes a matter for the courts. Many of the landlords and developers owe back taxes, so they do not want to fight it. Many of these buildings are full of artists and anarchists and minimum-wage workers. The people this city belongs to."

"That's one way to handle a housing crisis," Booker says.

"It is sometimes not ideal. There is no electricity, so the elevators don't work, but we have generators. No running water, but we're able to maintain a bathroom facility on the first floor. Which is why your ability to climb the stairs says where you live. The eldest get the ground floor."

As we reach the fifth level I'm getting the tiniest bit winded, which is the only thing keeping me from telling Enzo that I love everything about what they're doing.

Fighting back against the machine that takes everything.

It's not lost on me that I used to be part of that machine. The Agency was never about the mission Ravi sold me on—keeping the world spinning in the right direction. It was about making sure the people in power stayed in power, and got even richer along the way.

Enzo stops on the landing of the sixth floor, where a spindly young man with a mop of brown hair, probably no more than fifteen, is smoking a cigarette. He sees Enzo and immediately attempts to stamp it out, but Enzo pulls him close and whispers in his ear. The boy runs off.

"He should be in school," Enzo says, as we continue the climb.

"So you run the place," Booker says.

"Mostly, yes," he says. "We have a board, to consider and approve applications. We charge a very nominal rent that goes toward supply and upkeep. The rest of the money comes from my . . ." he pauses, searching, "side hustle, I guess you would say."

"So, how did you and Booker meet?" I ask.

Both Booker and Enzo stop and fix me with a hard stare. I put my hands up. "Sorry, shouldn't have asked."

They both nod, and we continue the climb in silence.

I guess there's some *there* there.

At the top of the stairs we step into a massive, almost opulent space—an open-concept apartment, with a bed and a kitchen and a lounge area. The furniture is mismatched, but in a tasteful way, like there's some intent behind the chaos. The only obstruction to the view out the floor-to-ceiling windows is a dozen support columns.

"Nice digs," Booker says.

Enzo laughs. "Indeed. Now, as a stickler for hospitality, I would again like to offer you a drink before we get started."

"It's appreciated, but time is of the essence," I tell him.

He leads us across the space to a doorway in the back, which has a heavy padlock on it. He turns it up toward him and keys in a combination, then slides a panel aside and presses his thumb to it.

He opens the door and stands back, letting us go inside. The lights flicker on and the room is covered in fencing and hooks, with enough guns to invade a small country. Everything from pistols to fully automatic assault rifles, and I'd be lying if I said it didn't give me goose bumps. Used to be walking into a room like this, for me, was like a kid walking into a toy store. Worse was I had enough money to get whatever I wanted.

But now, I'm severely limited in what I can and can't use.

Enzo closes the door. At the center of the room is a large

stainless-steel table, on which there's a small black zipped case, and three shrink-wrapped bundles of heavy fabric.

"Ilha da Queimada Grande," Enzo says. "I had heard rumors of what President Azevedo built there, and I suppose if that's where you're headed, those rumors are true." He unzips the case, opens it, and slides it forward, revealing two injectors. "Antivenom. This was the best I could do on short notice. The venom of the golden lancehead pit viper is hemotoxic, not neurotoxic. That means their bite won't paralyze you, but it will inflict massive tissue damage and internal hemorrhaging. If bitten, simply inject yourself near the bite, and try to ride out the pain." He holds up a finger. "Snakes will sometimes deliver what is called a dry bite, in which no venom is injected. So be judicious with the use of these."

"How will we know the difference between a live and a dry bite?" I ask.

Enzo's face goes dark. "You will know." Then he nudges the bundles of fabric. "Leg gaiters. Made from high-strength ballistic fiber and polyester. Not much, but a little insurance."

I pull the case toward me and examine the injectors. "How much?"

"Best we tabulate at the end. Now, please"—he holds his arms up—"you gentlemen are welcome to peruse, and I will answer any questions you may have."

We nod and the three of us wander around the space, examining the wares. It's a little difficult, as we're limited to nonlethal weapons only. But I quickly find a twenty-six-inch friction baton, which feels good in my hand—light, with a solid grip. And a tactical knife with a four-inch M4 steel blade. Not that I plan on opening any throats, but knives are good for more than just that. I place the two on the table and continue shopping.

I find a collection of Taser-style weapons, but those are out. Too easy to induce cardiac arrest. I'm starting to lose hope when I find a box of what looks like miniature road flares.

"Ah," Enzo says. "PepperBlasters." He takes one out and points it away from him. "I would demonstrate, but in this small space, it would not be a good idea. Each one delivers three shots of powder. Eight-pound trigger pull, ten-foot effective range. Reloadable, too." He hangs it from the front of his shirt. "Even has a clip."

"Perfect," I tell him, taking the box and placing it down next to the rest of my gear.

Next to that, Booker is fiddling with a shotgun with an orange fore-end, the words LESS LETHAL written down the stock. He's got a couple of boxes of rounds to go with it.

"We are walking softly on this one," Enzo says.

Me and Booker look at each other. It would be easy enough to explain our situation. But I think we both understand that there's no denying the protection our reputations provide us.

"No doubt, you will be shot at," Enzo says, disappearing into a corner. He comes back with three bulletproof vests, placing them on the table.

"What ballistic level?" I ask.

"Ballistic two, stab one," he says.

"Anything bigger than a nine-mil is going to cut right through that."

Enzo shrugs. "Best I have in stock."

"All right, well, I think this is what we came for." I turn to look for Lavigne. "You good?"

Lavigne steps out of the shadows with a baseball bat hefted over his shoulder.

"That's it?" I ask him.

He nods while holding eye contact.

"Okay, man, hard core," I tell him, then turn to Enzo. "What's the damage here, bud?"

Enzo looks at the table, then at us. "Had it not been for the antivenom, I would have offered this for free. A trade. That was quite expensive to procure, especially so quickly. I will give you those for cost, and the rest gratis, if you would do me one kindness."

"What's that?" I ask.

He takes out his phone, taps the screen a few times, and holds it up. The three of us crowd around him. It's a shot of a handsome man with long flowing hair and a thin beard. Enzo is embracing him, kissing him on the cheek.

"My partner, Domingo," he says. "He leads a group that opposes President Azevedo. He went missing about four months ago. If he is alive, I suspect that's where he would be."

"Why do you suspect that?" I ask.

Enzo shrugs. "Intuition. If this is truly Azevedo's baby, it's where he would keep him. I believe Domingo is too valuable to kill. But I also just . . ." He looks down, then back up to me, his eyes watering. "I just believe he is alive."

I put my hand on his shoulder. "If he's there, we'll find him and bring him back."

"Thank you," he says. "The, uh . . ." He clears his throat. "The antivenom cost ten thousand . . ."

I take the wad of cash out of my pocket, peel it off. "USD?"

He nods. "Thank you."

"And thank you for the rest—" I start.

I'm interrupted by a knock at the door. Enzo crosses over and cracks it open, and after listening to a hushed whisper says, "Tell them to wait."

More whispering. Enzo sighs.

"Fine, five minutes," he says, and closes the door, then turns to us. "Gentlemen, I am very sorry, I have more customers. I would have preferred to keep them downstairs, but my assistant . . ." He shrugs.

Enzo tosses us each a knapsack and we pack our gear as quickly as we can, and then step out into the apartment.

Standing across the room, his face half-wrapped in bandages, is Balor.

He doesn't seem surprised to see us.

"Isn't this grand," he says.

"You two know each other?" Enzo asks, with a confused grin.

V

If I show up at your door, chances are you did

something to bring me there.

—MARTIN Q. BLANK,

GROSSE POINT BLANK

ASTRID

Barcelona
Four Years Ago

The sky is a blazing orange that fades to indigo over our heads, a gentle breeze coming off the placid waters of the Balearic Sea. We've sailed out far enough the shoreline has disappeared, which makes me a little nervous. I don't like not knowing the best escape route.

But that shouldn't be a problem. No one's supposed to die today.

A model-pretty woman in a white polo shirt offers us a tray filled with blinis, topped with dollops of crème fraîche and generous mounds of glossy black caviar. Chea picks one off and stuffs it in her mouth. As the woman walks away, Chea scrunches her face and furrows her brow.

"Not for you?" I ask.

Chea swallows. "Rich people eat weird shit."

"That they do," I tell her, surveying the crowd of people

packing the deck of the mega yacht. Women in airy, impossibly expensive dresses, men in designer summer suits and boat shoes.

Somewhere amongst them is Anatol Kulesh, a Belarusian oligarch who is, according to our sources, that country's point person on the black-market weapons trade, selling to countries like Sudan, Myanmar, China, and Azerbaijan. He uses his yacht *Nadzeye* to meet with clients.

Which is why we're here.

I'm the head of a hedge fund and Chea is my assistant, invited to an evening cocktail party for international power brokers, by an Agency contact close to Kulesh's inner circle.

I slide my hand into my Jimmy Choo clutch, fingering the strip containing a dozen microphones; bleeding-edge tech courtesy of the Agency. Each one is the size of a lentil and transmits on a frequency that should evade most bug sweepers.

It's a simple enough gig. And Chea's first. Seemed like a good way to get her feet wet.

"So," Chea says, "I thought you said it wasn't like this."

"Like what?"

"Sneaking around. Dressing up."

Chea is wearing a Reem Acra V-neck gown, cream-colored with sequined silver tendrils reaching around it like bolts of lightning. It cost four thousand dollars, which was twice the cost of my black Oscar de la Renta minidress. And hers, I can't expense to the Agency.

But when we went to Bergdorf, the way her eyes lit up when she saw it, I couldn't say no.

The girl deserves something nice.

"It is very rarely like this," I tell her. "But when it is, you have to enjoy it."

Another waiter walks by with a tray of champagne. I pluck off two glasses and hand one to Chea. Her eyes dart around, like someone might come snatch it out of her hand. She leans into me. "I'm eighteen."

"You're almost nineteen," I tell her. "Live a little. But you're only getting the one."

"Should we be drinking when we work?" she asks.

"Sometimes you have to sit at a bar and blend in, and you can't blend in without a drink. When that's the case, drink one, then move on to water. In a rocks glass if you can manage it, because then it looks like you're drinking vodka."

I tip my glass back and take a sip, and she does the same. She smiles and puts her hand over her mouth. "Bubbly."

"Welcome to the high life, kid," I tell her, then look around. "Okay, these bozos look appropriately wasted. I'm going to get to work. You get some food, enjoy yourself, and if anyone hits on you, you just give 'em a stiff elbow overboard. Got it?"

She gives me a salute. "Got it."

"And do not take a second one of those," I say, nodding toward the glass.

"It's okay," she says. "I don't really have a taste for it."

"For the best," I tell her. Chea turns to work her way through the crowd on her Prada ballet flats. She wanted heels, but another rule of this job is: you never wear heels when you're working. Even on a gig like this. You never know when you're going to need to run.

As I watch her go, I wonder again if this is a good idea.

Then I put my fears aside, and move toward the interior of the boat, away from the crowds, looking for spots to plant the microphones.

Chea has been committed. She started watching hitman movies for "research," she said. I told her they were all make-believe, like watching *The Lord of the Rings* if you wanted to learn about European history.

She asked for her own gun, and the answer was a clear and forceful *no*. But I did consent to teaching her how to strip and clean my firearms. That felt like a good place to start; to teach her an appreciation for the weaponry. Like a monk sweeping the floors for a few years before they're allowed to meditate.

The first time she worked on my Glock 19, she was all thumbs, but within a week she had it stripped down and reassembled like she built the thing. She's a natural.

I'm not letting her kill anyone until she turns twenty-one, which is still older than I was, but seems fair.

It has been making me think about the way our trauma prepared us for this job. We're hypervigilant; constantly aware of our own surroundings, including other people. And we are deeply suspect of all men.

I find a staircase and head down into a living area—a circular room with floor-to-ceiling windows, an array of couches that look like they've never been sat on, and a fully stocked bar. I plant a microphone underneath the countertop of the bar, and then another in the bathroom, before making my way to the rear deck.

There's a tall man looking out over the ocean, his back to

me. I'm about to leave when he turns and catches me with the corner of his eye.

"Hello," he says.

I don't want to make him suspicious, so I go to the railing and lean on it, dangling my champagne glass over the water. Just below us is the boat's life raft. It looks like an inflatable speedboat, meant to fit in with the aesthetic of the rest of the ship.

"This is amazing, isn't it," I say.

"Da," he says.

He's Russian, well over six feet, and built like a jet fighter. He's wearing a navy suit with a white T-shirt underneath and a pair of shiny brown loafers. His head is shaved, but it looks good on him. He downs the last of his champagne and tosses the empty glass out onto the water and turns fully to me.

And he smiles.

It's not a bad smile. Though there's something familiar about his face . . .

"Dare to dream," he says. "That one day we might have toys like this."

I laugh. "One day."

"How do you know Anatol?" he asks.

"I don't, really," I say, finishing my glass, and placing it on a table next to us. "Just here networking. I run a hedge fund. Hudson Street Holdings. Hoping to make some inroads into some new markets."

The man nods. "I would introduce you to Anatol. He is an old friend."

"But . . . ?"

He raises an eyebrow. "Then he is going to steal you away, and where will that leave me?"

Ah, there it is. I consider cutting the conversation short, heading upstairs to check on Chea. But we have time to kill before we head back to port. Part of me doesn't want to draw suspicion to us—and the other part doesn't want to begrudge myself a little harmless flirting.

"So what do you do?" I ask.

He looks back out at the ocean. "Security. It is how I know Anatol."

"You look like the type."

"What type is that?" he asks.

"Like you can handle yourself."

He starts to say something, then stops.

"What?" I ask.

"Just, my heart is heavy."

"Why's that?"

He leans against the railing, bowing his head, no longer making eye contact. "It is my brother. He died five years ago. I miss him." He waves his hand toward the darkening sky. "Especially in moments like this. We grew up in Kamchatka. Do you know where that is?"

"That's about as far east in Russia as you can get. Pretty much the end of the world."

"Da. It is cold, and it is rough." He smiles, recalling the memory of it. "But it is *beautiful*. When we were boys, our father would take us out on the Icha river, every year in August. A little, tiny boat that we were always bailing water out of."

He gestures behind him, to the gleaming interiors of the yacht. "Nothing like this. We would spend days there, camping or sleeping on the boat. It is among the best memories I have of him. I hoped that one day we might return to it. Now he is gone."

"I'm so sorry. Can I ask how he died?"

The man looks up at me, his voice taking on a diamond edge. "He was killed."

My stomach flutters. That familiar feeling, looking at his face, takes on a darker tone. Something at the back of my brain telling me this was a mistake, that I'm being careless . . .

"It's nice to finally meet you, Astrid," he says. "Or should we keep this professional, and I can call you Azrael?"

That snatches the air out of my lungs.

He's not carrying a gun. I would have noticed that right off. There could be a knife in there, but I've got a folding karambit strapped to the inside of my thigh. I take a step back, to give myself a little distance in case I need it, and set my feet.

"You know my name," I say. "I still don't know yours."

He puts his hands behind his back, puffing out his chest, fully devoid of fear.

"Kozlov."

Atlantic City.

"How . . ." I start.

"Many pieces were moved into place," he says. "Many favors called upon. You see, it is not just that you killed my brother, it is that you took his property. And as his last surviving relative, anything he owned is passed down to me . . ." He looks past me, into the boat, and says, "Ah, here we are."

There are three men in the living area now, and a fourth coming through the doorway, leading Chea at gunpoint.

Kozlov has taken a few steps back, to a safer distance, and gestures to them.

"Please," he says. "Join us."

I step inside and meet eyes with Chea. I expect to see terror, but instead find resolve. She gives me a slight nod, as another man crosses the room and hands a gun to Kozlov. He smiles as he accepts it, and Anatol steps through the doorway.

He's a stout man, built like an old-school boxer, with a miserably bad toupee. He looks at Chea, looks at me, and crosses the room to Kozlov. They huddle and speak to each other in hushed tones.

After a moment, Anatol nods, and without regarding us, exits the room.

"So what now?" I ask.

It's a dumb question, but I need a few seconds to situate myself. There are four men now, one holding Chea. The other two don't appear to be armed. Four men and two guns . . .

"Now, you will meet your eternal rest, at the bottom of the Balearic," Kozlov says. "Your friend here will join me, as my traveling companion . . ."

Chea raises her eyebrow. The man holding the gun on her, he's standing too close. That's the mistake people make, holding someone else at gunpoint. We've done disarm drills, over and over, but it's different when it's a live-fire situation versus a rubber training gun.

Don't do it, I want to tell her. *Let them kill me. Get away. You're strong enough now. Once you're back on land, once you're safe . . .*

I try to communicate this through a look and I can't tell if she doesn't understand, or if she's ignoring me, because she leans forward, sobbing loudly into her hands. It draws everyone's attention, which gives me just enough time to throw a foot into Kozlov's midsection, sending him backward over the couch, the gun flying into a corner.

I glance over my shoulder at Chea—she's dipped to the side and managed to get the man's gun away from him, and she swings the butt of it in a tight arc toward his face, smashing his nose. I pull the karambit out from its sheath just as one of the other men makes it to me, and I rake it across his throat, a hot gush of blood spraying across my face, getting into my mouth.

I turn to Kozlov and hear a gunshot behind me; Chea has shot the other man in the shoulder. He goes down, screaming in pain. But the distraction is just enough for Kozlov to grab me from behind and lift me up, knocking the knife from my grasp.

He gets me perpendicular to him, practically over his head, probably to bring my spine down on his knee, so I wrap my arm around his neck, stopping my momentum, and causing him to jerk forward. We topple into a pile and I throw a foot into his jaw. It's not a good shot, but it's enough to create some space.

Chea is struggling with the man whose nose she broke; he's got her down on the couch, his hands wrapped around her neck. She's swinging at him but doesn't have any leverage. I try to give her some, kicking him in the back of the leg to bring him down to his knees.

I turn to Kozlov, who is now up and squared to me. We circle each other for a moment, before I hear it.

Screaming.

Someone must have heard the gunshot. Anatol is a gun-runner; probably half the people on this boat are strapped.

Chea is back up, the gun in her hand again. I hold my hand out and she tosses it at me, just as Kozlov dives for cover. I fire a couple of shots as I run toward the rear of the boat, Chea following, and I yell over my shoulder, "Jump."

I vault over the railing, feel the gentle sea air on my skin before I make contact with the deck of the lifeboat. Chea lands besides me as I'm detaching the tether. The key is already in the ignition. The engine roars as I steer it away from the yacht and look up, to see a group of people standing at the railing. Gunshots slice the air around us, pelting the water. Just as I pull Chea down and out of firing range, I see Kozlov—the tallest of them, so the easiest to pick out—lob something over his head toward us.

I hear it land but I don't see it. I push Chea away from me, over the side of the boat, and leap into the water just as the explosion hits.

The shock wave sends me sprawling under the waves. I expect the initial pain of the blast to subside but it doesn't; salt water screams into my skin, from my shoulder blade down to my lower back.

I grab something that's floating, I don't even know what, and look around the darkening water for Chea, as the yacht's engines turn on and it drifts away from us. Of course Anatol will want to get as far from this as possible.

I scream for Chea, but it's dark and overcast now, and I can barely see more than a hundred feet. My grip on the debris is slipping. I slide my hand to my watch and click the button on the side. The emergency-use homing beacon that'll send someone from the Agency to come out and get me.

And as I float there, my body racked with pain, I call Chea's name into the pitch-black night until my voice goes hoarse.

ASTRID

The Tenth Circle
Now

How do you break out of a prison?

Putting aside the litany of things working against me here: you need to understand the layout and security, you need to understand the routines, and you need some kind of assistance, whether that be from someone on the inside, or the outside.

With not much else to do aside from my interrogation sessions, I walk the parts of the prison that are open to me. The rec area, the outdoor courtyard, the cafeteria, some of the hallways. A few times I come across an owl who sets their feet and projects an aura of *turn around,* so I do.

There are cameras everywhere except in the showers. There are microphones recording and analyzing what we say, with only one dead zone I can be sure of, in the yard. There are thirty-two inmates and twenty guards to a shift, all of them armed with stun sticks. They probably have access to heavier weaponry, too. We don't have the numbers.

We have no access to outside communication. Anything that could be useful is kept in restricted areas. The guards won't make the mistake of carrying their phones. Not after Godfrey.

I want to get out. I don't want anyone to die in the process. Even if I tried to sow a little chaos, incite a riot so I could get outside, then people could get killed. Guards or inmates. I don't want that to happen.

What if I could get outside? Would it even make a difference? Then I have to swim. And I don't even know for sure which direction.

I've considered finding a way to approach Domingo, see if I can get some kind of radio or cell phone, something that'll let me make contact with the outside world. I'm not sure if Mark and the others are still alive, and I question whether I should continue to draw them into this.

What else?

The doctor has a dead man's switch in his chest that will leave the entire population here to the elements if he's killed.

That's one thing. But the other thing is, he has a daughter.

We're about twenty-five miles off the coast, which is, what, ten minutes in a helicopter? But helicopters are expensive. That's fuel and manpower, and what if they're undergoing maintenance, or they can't fly because of the weather? What if he needed to get out of here quickly? Dr. Vogt is a father. He seems to love his daughter. He would want a faster way off the island. A backup plan, just in case the helicopter isn't available.

I know I would. It's only something I've thought about a million times in the past few years.

I would put good money on there being a boat somewhere on the island.

Great—if it's true, and if I could figure out how to get to it. The security here is good but it's not exactly James Bond–level shit. There are cracks.

Saving my ass, and removing whatever thing they're trying to dig out of my head, seems like a priority. But that means there'll be thirty-one prisoners left behind here. Do all of them deserve to be here? Maybe. But nothing about this place says rehabilitation. It's punishment. At the hands of a doctor who's going to use them like playthings, smiling like a kid the whole time.

It'd be easy enough to just get up and go. The real problem is Yumei.

Leaving her is the thing that's making this hard. She's here because of me. I owe her an amends, at the very least, and leaving her here to rot seems like the opposite of that. Further punishment.

If I'm going to take her, then I need to give everyone the opportunity to leave. In Assassins Anonymous you have to draw your own lines, and that's the line I want for myself. And yes, maybe some of them are going to go back out and do bad things, but they ought to have a choice. There's no choice here. If you have a choice, you can make the choice to be better.

So what have I got?

I've got a rough sense of the layout, which is a pretty good start. The routines of the guards don't seem regular. But a new shift comes in every few days. We're locked in our rooms at night. During the day there are always a half dozen or more in eyeshot, the rest floating around the facility.

The only way to make this work would be to take them out all at once.

There's no way to escape by my lonesome. This has to be a team effort. It makes me think about the AA meetings. Sitting there and listening. Never sharing. I want to say that it's because I'm not ready, because I'm waiting for the right time. The truth is, I don't want to vomit my traumas all over everyone. They're mine to carry. They always have been. It's my responsibility.

The only way I get out of here is by letting that go.

So I do the thing Mark would encourage me to do.

Remember that I'm not alone.

I make it to the dining hall and see the prisoners just starting to tuck in to their meals. As per usual, Quraishi is sitting by himself, off in the corner. Out of earshot of anyone. I go and get a tray and load it with food, not even paying attention to what I'm putting on it, then carry it over and sit across from him.

The program. Think about the program.

It's what Mark would say to me right now.

That you only need two people for a meeting.

Quraishi looks at me as I sit.

"I'm sorry," I tell him. "I shouldn't have spoken to you so harshly."

He shrugs. Whether it's forgiveness or indifference, I can't tell.

"My name is Astrid," I say. "I haven't killed anyone in a year and . . . six months, I think."

He tilts his head a little.

"Assassins Anonymous," I say, "is a group of men and women who try to help each other recover, using their shared experience, strength, and a bit of hope. The only requirement for membership is a desire to stop. Our primary purpose is to stop killing and help others to achieve the same."

"This is not where I expected this conversation to go," he says. Then he adds: "You know who I was."

"Yes, and you may have known me as Azrael," I say.

I know we're not supposed to do that, but it feels like a peace offering.

He nods but doesn't seem to betray any knowledge of who I was. I'm not sure if that makes me happy or disappointed.

"In a normal recovery program it's about an understanding that there's a power greater than yourself, and it can be whatever you want it to be. Assassins Anonymous reframes it slightly, as a reminder that we aren't gods. Because we acted as if we were. That the right to take a life was ours to decide. We have to surrender our egos."

Quraishi looks around the cafeteria, mindful of the microphones transcribing our every word. "So what would you do?" he asks. "Next?"

"Next we would . . . talk," I tell him, even though that's never what I really did. It's a little funny, too, because the day I was taken, the walk to the church, I was psyching myself up. Telling myself, *Today is the day. I'm going to share.*

Instead I felt some relief when I was sitting in the back of that van, a hood over my head.

Realizing, *Now I don't have to be vulnerable.*

Right now it's the only thing that might save me.

"Could be about the way we were," I tell him. "Could be about what's hard today. Could be anything, really. I think that's the point. I have a sponsor, Mark, and he says that we never had to have the hard conversations in our line of work. We did our job and we moved on. Being able to talk about it is a good first step."

Quraishi leans back in his seat and looks around, like he's making sure we're still alone. Then he takes the small cup that had been filled with chocolate pudding and sets about scraping the sides, just to get a little more.

He points the spoon at me and says, "I think it is interesting to explore these feelings in the context of a recovery program. I can see"—he sticks the spoon in his mouth and pulls it back out—"how what we did was addictive."

"Apparently there are similarities in brain structure between addicts and killers. Impulse control, stuff like that. But honestly, I just think it feels good to be good at something, and we were very good at the things we did. Within that skill set we found reward, and then righteousness. At least, I did . . ."

"You know who I am," he says. "You know the things I've done. If not in detail, at least in spirit. And I could sit here and tell you why I did them, but I won't. I am past the point of that." He puts down the pudding cup. "I would like to tell you about a wedding."

I throw him a curious little glance.

He looks down at his hand, and when he sees that I've followed, he traces letters on the tabletop.

B-R-O-T-H-E-R.

"He saw the world for what it could be. I saw the world for what it wasn't. He loved me, despite everything. When he told me he was to marry, he asked me not to attend. It was the only time I ever broke a promise to him. I needed to be there. I watched, from afar. And do you know what I saw?"

"What?" I ask.

"Happiness like I have never known," he says, his voice growing soft and wistful. "My entire life I have been fighting wars. Some real, some imagined. All of them, within myself. I never stopped, never took a moment to look around. Never saw what joy could look like. What it could taste like or sound like. And that day I saw joy. The men and the women and the children. Dancing and laughing and eating. It made me realize not just the things I had lost for myself, but the thing I had taken from so many others."

"So what did you do?"

He shrugs.

"I walked away. From all of it. I decided that the only war that mattered was the one in my heart and I would continue to fight, but I would not shatter another life." He laughs. "Two months later I was captured. I suspect I lost my resolve. My focus."

"And now you're here."

"And now I'm here," he says. "I do not expect you to believe this, but I deeply regret the things I have done. Once I removed myself from the haze of anger, I could see more clearly. I still harbor deep resentments toward those who have killed and enslaved my people in the name of a god or a dollar. But I see what I did: I perpetuated a cycle of violence. I fed the machine. I am just as much to blame. I was not a victim, nor a martyr."

"Let go and let god," I tell him. "Something Mark likes to say."

He nods without me having to explain it. "Exactly."

I lightly tap the table, until he looks down at my fingers. I slowly trace the letters:

E-S-C-A-P-E.

He shakes his head at me. "Impossible," he says softly.

B-O-A-T.

"Maybe," he says.

The next part I have to risk saying out loud; I don't know if I can communicate it to him.

"The guards," I say. "The injection sites on their arms. Do you know what they are?"

"I have only suspicion," he says, his eyes narrowed. He traces on the table, a jumble of letters I lose track of halfway through. When I shake my head at him, he does it again, slower.

M-I-T-H-R-I-D-A-T-I-S-M.

Oh. That makes sense. Mithridatism is when you build a tolerance to a poison by receiving tiny doses of the poison. Does that work with snake venom?

"I have had a great deal of time to think about this," Quraishi says. "Maybe it works, maybe the doctor is simply testing a hypothesis. I cannot think of anything else it would be."

The plan is formulating in my head. If there's a way I can screw with the injections, then maybe it would be possible to take out all the guards in one fell swoop.

"I wonder," Quraishi says, "if you have been given a work assignment yet."

He has a sly smile on his face. I think he gets what I'm thinking.

"Many of the prisoners here have work assignments," he says. "Perhaps you haven't gotten one because you are currently the subject of the doctor's more focused experiments. But, for example, I am responsible for the library. There are prisoners who work in the cafeteria. And some who work in the medical office."

"Sounds like a nice gig," I say. "I wonder who works that one?"

He nods toward the other end of the cafeteria, where Yumei is currently boring a hole into me.

Well.

I guess it makes sense.

The only way for me to make this plan work is to make an amends.

And hope she doesn't kill me in the process.

MARK

alor steps forward and smiles, spreading his arms like he wants me to hug him. He's flanked by two men in light tactical gear—cargo pants and heavy boots and thin bullet-proof vests under their shirts. Both of them are built out of weathered bricks and covered with tattoos. They look like they were ordered from a mercenary catalog, and the only real difference between them is that one has a shock of wild hair and a bushy beard, while the other is shorn smooth. No eyebrows even.

"I thought I might run into you again," Balor says. Then he tugs down the camouflage gaiter around his neck, revealing a patch of burnt, mottled skin, covered in bandages and seeping blood. "I owe you for this, don't I now?"

Enzo steps between us. "Gentlemen. I know how quickly these pissing contests can spiral out of control. There are innocent people in this building and I respectfully ask that you take this elsewhere."

"Oh, there are no gentlemen here," Balor says, holding eye contact with me. "Just a bunch of stone-cold killers."

Booker slides up and drops his voice so only I can hear. "How we going to play this one?"

I know the answer, even though I don't want to tell him.

A year and a half ago I was lying on the floor of a luxury penthouse apartment, and a man named Kozlov was standing over me, pointing a gun at my chest. I thought that was it. The end of my life. The penance I would pay for all the lives I've taken.

And then a sword erupted from his chest.

It was Kenji, giving up six years of sobriety to save my life. He was almost immediately shot for his trouble, and he died in my arms.

As he went, he said, *It's okay.*

That's it.

It's okay.

I think about that a lot. What exactly he meant. It was a little obtuse, in the context, but I'm pretty sure he meant that what he gave up, he gave gladly to protect me. The sacrifice he was making as my sponsor, and as my friend.

In recovery programs, there are two kinds of amends: a regular amends and a living amends, where you commit to living a sober lifestyle. I think, in Assassins Anonymous, there's a third kind of amends.

An amends of last rites.

If I have to take out Balor, and maybe die in the process, but it frees up Booker and Lavigne to save Astrid—that works for me.

I'll bear it.

I don't want to.

But I will, because I can.

"How about this," I tell Balor. "Rather than risk hurting people, you and me throw down. Right here, right now. Just us. Your boys stand down, so do mine, and everyone agrees to accept the outcome. You get to see how tough you are."

A look passes between him and his two partners. I can't tell what kind of look it is. Maybe a little fear? That he has to stand on his own two feet for this one? Maybe that's just wishful thinking.

He nods and smiles. "Let's go, then."

"Enzo," I say, "can we use the roof? Keep this confined?"

Enzo sighs and points us toward the stairwell. "Best-case scenario, I guess."

As I turn, Booker grabs my arm, digging his fingers into my biceps.

"This isn't the way," he says.

"Decision is made," I tell him. "If he kills me, you two go get her."

We make our way to the roof. Mercifully, it's still overcast. At least I don't have to deal with the glare. The roof is completely bare, save a set of cheap lawn furniture in the far corner, moldering in the elements. There's a waist-high wall surrounding the edge.

Hard to feel like this doesn't end with one of us taking a tumble.

Balor is stripping down now, pulling off his T-shirt to reveal a tank top. He's covered in rippling muscles, and tattoos stretching from his forearms, up and around his shoulder blades. There are bandages too—a lot of them. Ms. Nguyen was right; don't see a body, assume they're not dead.

"I have to tell you," Balor says, "I wondered if you might be here. The only major weapons dealer in the city who works with our lot. Pretty smart, no?"

"Brilliant. If you manage to take me out, I imagine your employers will be happy."

He smirks. "Oh, she doesn't care. At this point, I'm flying solo. It's personal." He waves his hand around the bandages. "As you can imagine."

Balor moves to the center of the roof, and I follow. The cheering section stays back, Enzo and Booker and Lavigne now standing with the other two men, their grievances forgotten. I pull off my shirt, too, feeling the twinge in my damaged shoulder as I do. My boots are heavy, so I kick them off, then bend down and take my socks off, and roll up the cuffs of my pants.

I got the measure of Balor on our first fight. He's brutal, fast, but he moves in straight lines. I need to circle more, stay light on my feet. Get him angry. The angrier he gets, the stupider he'll get.

The surface of the roof is rough under my bare feet, but it feels good, too. Balor hasn't removed his shoes, and he's hopping around now like a boxer, shaking out his arms, putting on a show.

Accept the things we cannot change, and all that.

Part of the reason I moved to the roof is that there's nothing around us he can use as a weapon, aside from gravity. I stretch my back, trying to conjure that feeling that used to live at my core, that black smoke that would consume everything around it and shoot me through with god-energy when I took a life.

My greatest weapon.

But just as I'm on the edge of finding it, dusting it off and turning it loose, I decide to go another way.

All that ever did was make me into something I don't want to be anymore, and if I'm going to do this, I'm going to do it as Mark, not as the Pale Horse. Even if I get killed, I'm going into this fight with the final vestiges of my integrity intact.

Balor comes at me fast, his shoulders cocked out and spread wide, which makes me think he's trying to distract me, get me to look up, so he can snap a kick out at my legs, which he does, and I check it with my shin.

Upon landing I take a big step forward and hinge my knee into his stomach. He manages to arch his midsection back, so he doesn't take all of it. Then he throws a snappy hook into my side, catching me right below my kidney.

Pain ripples through my side and I hop back, try to create some space between us and reset myself, but he doesn't let up, coming at me with a snappy kick that I just barely manage to step away from.

Then he's throwing shots that I'm struggling to keep up with. It's pure defense at this point, until he manages to catch me on the chin with his fist, and even though it's not clean, I can feel it, knocking at the door.

The Pale Horse, begging to be let out.

I push the door closed.

From there it's a flurry, back and forth, the two of us trying to gain the upper hand. He lands some good shots; I get a few in as well. It doesn't take long until we're both a little winded, and we move back to give each other space, so we can breathe and look for a smarter way into this.

"Really thought you'd be a better time," Balor says.

The problem is, I'm fighting half-cocked. I've seen six different ways to kill him since I started.

No, the problem is that I'm *fighting*.

I need to stop thinking of myself as a weapon, honed and sharpened to kill, so I imagine myself standing near the statue of Dr. Sun Yat-sen, with Master Feng leading us through a gentle tai chi practice.

Don't struggle with the energy.

Just move it around.

Balor comes at me again, but this time, rather than meet the attack with a counter, I move offline at the last second, sliding to his dead side and letting him stumble past me. He whips around to find me standing and waiting.

The next time he comes at me, I get light on my toes, moving away from his strikes. He lands a few, but they're glancing. Mostly he's swinging at the air. He gets desperate, each subsequent blow harder, more desperate, but that makes them easier to see, and soon I'm dancing around him, lost in the rhythm of my feet gliding on the roof.

Furious, he throws a massive push kick at me, but I grab his foot under the ankle and hop back, breaking his stance, then throw it hard to my right, sending him to the ground. He gets on his hands and knees and pounds his fists on the roof, screaming now, seeing red.

Good.

Red means stupid.

He comes at me again, but now he's slower. The tank is running empty. Still, I need a way to end this. Tiring him out will only do so much. I move in tandem with him, flowing around him, moving him toward the edge of the roof.

When we get close, I let him land a few shots, think he has the upper hand. Keep him cocky, keep him distracted. I falter a little, like maybe I'm hurt and trying to recover. He tries to take advantage of this, throwing a wide haymaker that, if it connected, would probably knock my teeth out.

It doesn't connect.

I move under it, getting close to his body, where I nudge him with my shoulder, using his momentum to send him toward the edge of the roof. Before he can fall backward, I grab his vest, making sure my grip is good. His feet are still on the lip but he's got no leverage.

He won't fall unless I let him.

But he can't get his footing, either.

Stalemate.

"I want you to listen to me," I tell him. "Are you listening?"

"Spare me the speech and just do it," he says, holding his arms out, his Christ-on-the-cross pose. Accepting his fate.

"No," I say, throwing him back onto the roof. He lands in a

pile but doesn't get up. I walk over and take a knee next to him. "I asked if you were listening to me. It's important that you are."

He breathes hard through his teeth but stays on the ground.

"You asked me why I don't kill anymore," I say. "The long story is that I did a fucked-up thing and hurt someone who didn't deserve it and it made me reconsider my relationship to the job. The reason I don't kill is because I *choose* not to kill. I get that letting you live is the harder way, because, yeah, you could turn right around and kill me."

He starts to say something, then stops himself.

"You wanted to kill me for the story, right?" I say, cocking my head back toward his friends. "The man who took down the Pale Horse. They can see I already won. If you want to perpetuate your own myth, you'll probably have to kill them, too. But none of it will matter." I get closer to him, and he could gut me if he wanted. "The truth is you lost. That won't change."

"That's it, then?" he asks.

"That's it. I used to bring death. Now, I grant you life. You choose what happens next."

I push myself to my feet, trying to hide the effort that takes, and I stand with my back to the edge of the roof. It would be so easy for him to get up and push me over. And I want him to see that I know that.

I don't need to die for Astrid and I don't need to kill this man.

All I need to do is live within my integrity.

This is what I've been unable to do. Why I'm here in the first place. What Ms. Nguyen has been trying to explain to me. Sometimes you need to let go. As men we're taught that every weight in the entire world needs to be piled on our backs, and we shouldn't dare show a crack. Shouldn't ever admit the effort. But sometimes the greatest freedom we can grant ourselves is putting some of it down.

I'm not responsible for Astrid's recovery, or her life. I still want to save it. I still want to live, too. I want to get through this without killing Balor. But all this struggle has gotten me nothing but a sick feeling in the pit of my stomach.

It's time to let go and let god.

Balor gets up, and for a moment I think, *This is it*. He's going to kill me, take his win, and go on to tell his story.

He looks at me one last time, spits, shakes his head, and turns to leave, his cronies following behind him. I watch them descend the stairs until they disappear, followed by the sound of their footsteps.

Then it's just silence, and I allow myself to fall flat on my back, my vision swallowed by the sky. The pain comes crashing in, the adrenaline finally wearing off. I took a lot more damage in that fight than I realized.

Booker offers me his hand, pulling me to my feet. "Can't believe you talked that fool out of killing you."

Enzo appears at my side. "I have pain medications, if you would like. On the house, for the way you handled that."

"That would be great," I tell him, though I'll hold off on taking them. I need a clear head. "We could use something else. A lift to Guarujá."

"About an hour and a half by car," Enzo says, patting me on the shoulder. "I will take you myself."

"Thanks."

I stumble toward the stairway and catch Lavigne staring at me, his eyes searching. Curious.

"C'mon," I tell him. "Time to get our shit and go."

He pauses, like he wants to say something, but then he shakes his head and follows us toward the stairwell. The short walk down to Enzo's isn't pleasant—my shoulder aches and something is clicking in my knee.

Despite the pain, I feel content.

I made the right decision.

VI

Supreme excellence consists in breaking the enemy's resistance without fighting.

—Sun Tzu, *The Art of War*

ASTRID

Beijing
Two Years Ago

Another day.

Another rich asshole to kill.

My first gig back since Chea died, since Kozlov left me with two scars: one down my back, and a more indelible one across the surface of my heart.

Everything that followed Barcelona was a mess. The Agency stepped in to clean it up, but I have two strikes now, with Atlantic City. Doesn't matter how good my record has been otherwise—I suspect I won't get a third chance, so this needs to be clean.

The driver lets me out of the car on an empty roadway at the bottom of a hill. It's chilly, and I pull my mink shawl a little closer to my shoulders. In front of me there's a concrete wall with a black gate. I walk to the intercom and press the button. After a few seconds, the gate retracts.

It's nice to be back. Not just because I could use the distraction—I have some aggression to work out.

What doesn't feel good is the outfit. The black dress that's a little too short at the top and the bottom. The makeup, caked on so heavy I feel like a clown. The blond wig, making my scalp itch. It used to feel exciting, to do this. Playing dress-up, sneaking into places. Now it just underscores the way the Agency looks at me.

I should be happy that I got this job and the Pale Horse didn't, but whoever he is, I'm sure they can't dress him up like an escort.

The worst part is, I don't even get to hurt this guy.

And I want to hurt someone.

Declan Mather is a billionaire who does tech stuff. I knew who he was before I got this assignment, and I always wondered what that tech stuff was. It never seemed clear. An AI start-up, some kind of green energy initiative. He owns a lot of companies and talks a lot about innovation but doesn't really seem to innovate anything.

Then Ravi pulled me into his office last week and told me he had to go.

There were two caveats. It has to look natural—hence the syringe of oleander—and I have to make a copy of his hard drive, then wipe the computer.

Easy enough. In all the research and surveillance I did, Declan looks decently fit, but doesn't have any kind of fighting or security background. He's a long-distance runner, so he's in good shape, which means I have to be extra-careful about making sure the injection site is easy to miss. But Ravi said they'd do the best they could to grease the wheels at the hospital, so there won't be too much of an inquiry there.

As I climb the stairway to the front door, passing a shiny black Tesla, I wonder what kinds of sins this man has to atone for.

Doesn't matter. Even if I did get to kill him the fun way, it wouldn't do anything to calm this electric sizzle in my gut.

Months I've been looking for the Russian. I know he's Kozlov's brother. I don't even know his first name. But I do know he goes by the Beast, and he spent some time in Orenburg Oblast, also known as the Black Dolphin—probably the most infamous and brutal Russian prison, near the border of Kazakhstan. If you make it out of there alive you've been whittled to a razor-sharp point, so it's no wonder I can't find him.

But I will.

And I'm going to kill him very slowly. I've been brushing up on medieval torture techniques for ideas. So far I've narrowed it down to lingchi—death by a thousand cuts—in which I'll just string him up and slice him to pieces slowly. But boiling him alive is slipping in as my favorite. Records from the reign of Henry VIII indicate it took some people up to two hours to die from that method.

I just need to find a pot big enough . . .

The door opens, and Declan Mather is standing there, waiting for me, in a button-down blue shirt, slacks, and gold-toed socks. He's handsome, in a bit of a strange way. His face is rugged, his graying hair carefully sculptured. The size of his face is oddly proportioned. It's too long. Even more so when he smiles, contorting his features, even though it's a friendly smile.

"Jenny," he says.

"That's me," I tell him, walking into the house and putting on a grin that is probably not nearly as enthusiastic as it should be for the façade—but men never seem to notice that kind of thing.

He's about to say something but stops and takes his phone out of his pocket.

"I'm sorry, I really need to take this," he says, looking at the screen. Then he points across the room to a bar. "Please feel free to pour yourself a drink. I'll be done momentarily."

"Not a problem," I tell him, smiling with my mouth closed.

He steps into the darkened kitchen and I cross the sparsely furnished living room to the bar—a beautiful, antique wooden cabinet that is ridiculously well-stocked. I pick up a rye I've never heard of and pour myself a small taste of it as his words drift through the space. Even though he's keeping his voice down, it's hard not to make out what he's saying.

"This is not a good time . . . Yes, I understand that . . . I understand that . . . I'm sorry, I don't know what to tell you."

A moment passes.

"Thank you, Mr. Vice President."

Interesting. I throw back the rye and it stings in exactly the right way, then turn to find Declan standing in the doorway of the kitchen.

"That was terribly rude," he says. "I'm sorry."

"Like I said, not a problem," I tell him, putting my arms

behind me on the bar and leaning back. Exposing myself to him. Daring him to do something stupid.

To give me an excuse.

He smiles—a small, pained smile that seems to belie something he wants to say but doesn't feel brave enough to. Then he crosses the room to me and picks up a glass, plucks out the bottle I had taken a pour from. He gives me another taste and pours a few fingers for himself.

Up close, I get a good look at him, and try to figure the best way to bring him down and inject him. Generally the safest bet is a rear naked choke, compressing the arteries in his neck and cutting off the oxygen supply to his brain until he passes out. I just need to hit that sweet spot between passing out and dying. If he dies from strangulation, there'll be telltale signs—damage to his throat and airway, petechial hemorrhaging in his eyes. That's a little harder to cover up. Any first-year medical student would notice. Hell, a true-crime podcast fan might catch it.

Declan downs the entire glass in one go and says, "How are you going to do it?"

"Do what?"

"Kill me," he says, reaching across me to pour himself another drink.

I take a step back. "I don't know what you mean?"

"Please," he says. "It's okay. I knew this day was coming."

"How?" I ask, finally managing to find some words.

He pours me another glass and gestures toward the sitting area. He leans back in an armchair and I perch on the edge of the couch. I consider the whiskey, but put the glass down on the coffee table with a sharp *clack*.

He looks up at me and smiles. There's relief in the smile. "You're not an escort. You painted your nails yourself. You're wearing flats, not heels. Never seen a working girl wear flats. I've been through enough escorts to know the difference."

I lean forward, suddenly a little less angry and a lot more interested.

"You're not going to try and stop me?"

He takes his glass, sipping it slowly. "Do you know why I'm in Beijing?"

"This is where you stay when you're in town on business," I tell him. "But you didn't appear to have anything on your schedule, so we thought it might be a social visit . . ."

Then it dawns on me, and he sees it, smiling and pointing his glass at me.

"China won't extradite."

"No, it does not," he says. "I was playing a little chess. Some things I did . . . are about to come to light. Killing me on U.S. soil is hard. I'd probably get marched off to jail, and I don't want to go to jail. China offers deniability. Too far away for anyone to accept credit or blame."

"You're just going to let me do it, then?" I ask.

He sighs and leans forward, his forearms on his knees. "Have you ever done something so bad . . . and even though you knew it was bad, you just . . . couldn't help yourself? Like a boulder, rolling down a hill."

I open my mouth, Chea's name on my tongue, but stop. It would be so easy to unburden myself. To tell him what happened. How I was so careless, on so many levels. I don't know why I feel compelled to do that; maybe because he'll be dead in a few minutes. I haven't breathed a word of what happened to anyone. I've been sitting in my apartment for days at a time, staring at the wall, wondering what I could have—should have—done differently.

Maybe saying it out loud will help me get a better grasp of it.

But there's something unsettling about this man. A smoothness, meant to hide something darker.

"Why am I here?" I ask.

He registers surprise at this. "They didn't tell you?"

"They don't usually. Above my pay grade."

"How much am I worth?"

"Fifty."

"That's all?" He makes a *hmph* noise. "Thought I'd be worth more. So how did you plan on doing it?"

I reach under my dress, take out the syringe strapped to my thigh, and hold it up, making sure I'm not close enough that he can knock it from my hand. "Oleander. It won't come up on a regular tox screen. It'll look like a heart attack."

"Will it hurt?"

"Maybe a little."

He walks over to the bar, picks up the bottle of rye, and chugs a quarter of it. Then he walks back over and sits on the chair, pulling off his sock. "You should inject it somewhere that's easy to hide. Between my toes would be good."

Declan sits there, waiting, his toes spread and pointed to the ceiling. I get up and kneel in front of him, now suddenly less worried that he's trying to play me.

I can see it in his face.

He wants to die.

"Why?" I ask.

He grimaces. "I'm not brave enough to do it myself."

I take his foot and spread his two biggest toes apart and find a vein. He winces as I pierce the skin, then I press the plunger, and it's done. I sit back and place the needle back in its carrying case.

He slumps back.

That was not satisfying in the least.

I get up and move through the apartment, toward the study. It's down the hall and to the right; I checked the floor plan earlier today. I still have to make a copy of his hard drive.

There's a laptop on the desk, and I open it up. Password protected. It doesn't appear to have anything more elaborate than the manufacturer's built-in password enabled, which will take about five minutes to bypass. But it's got a fingerprint scanner on it. Maybe I can save myself some time. I bring it to the living room—Declan won't have been dead too long. We all have electricity running through our bodies, and these scanners use that to read the ridges and valleys of a finger-print. I hold the open laptop and take his hand and press a finger to it, and it opens.

Lucky me. Another couple of minutes and that probably wouldn't have worked.

There's a video in the center of the screen, paused on a young boy with a mop of brown hair, wearing a T-shirt with a baseball on it.

My stomach drops. I press the PLAY button, and someone off-screen is in mid-sentence, so I scroll it back.

"What's your name?" a voice asks. A woman.

"Tommy."

"And how old are you, Tommy?"

The boy looks a little nervous. "Twelve."

"So like I told you earlier, we're going to go to this island, this special island, where they have pools with slides and a big home theater and any kind of food you might ever want to eat. It's like a vacation."

"That sounds cool."

"But you're going to need a new swimsuit. Would you mind taking your shirt off for me, so I can get your measurements?"

The boy's smile drops, and he looks away. "Well . . ."

"It's just us," the woman says. "You can trust me."

"What about the camera?"

"Oh, it's not on . . ."

I stop the video.

And I want to empty the contents of my stomach all over Declan's dead body.

The island. Declan owns a thirteen-acre private island in the Grenadines. He's known for throwing big, lavish parties. Retreats for the rich and famous. And not just regular rich and famous. Presidents, princes, bank CEOs, oil barons.

I press my fingers to the side of his neck, just to be sure, like someone as monstrous as he is might be able to rise from the dead. I ball my fist and consider hitting him. Stabbing him. Ruining his face and his body. Destroying him. And the only reason I don't is because he won't feel it, and therefore it won't bring me any joy.

I take out the thumb drive Ravi gave me and insert it into the side of the laptop. I don't even have to do anything; it automatically copies the entire computer. A little box pops up on the screen that reads: THREE MINUTES.

The time passes by in a haze.

When it's done I consider getting up, but then I remember what he said in the kitchen.

Mr. Vice President.

And I wonder.

I click through the computer. It doesn't take long before I find a folder, PROSPECTS, and when I open it up, the screen is filled with thumbnail images, videos like the one I just saw. They're shrunken down so I can't make out the details but every one of them is a child standing against a blank wall. Against my better judgment I look at the bottom of the window, where it says there are 478 files in this folder.

I keep looking, until finally I see a folder labeled CLIENTS.

It's full of files. Each one is a name I recognize. The vice president. Two members of the British royal family. Russian oligarchs, Chinese government officials. Two A-list celebrities.

I pick the vice president's folder and open that. Another series of videos. I click on the first and it's an overhead shot of a massage table, a doughy man lying on his stomach, his bare ass out for the world to see.

A young girl enters.

I stop it. I don't need to see the rest.

I don't want to see the rest.

It's hard to believe how little security the laptop had—

especially for someone working in the tech sphere. It makes me wonder if Declan was stupid, or just that confident.

Maybe he wanted to get caught.

I pop out the thumb drive, hold it in my hand. The plastic creaks in my grip. It feels heavier than it should. Then I click through the control settings until I find the option to securely wipe the hard drive. I move the cursor until it's hovering over the START button.

And I wonder which person in that folder is the one who paid for me to be here.

The list is seared into my memory; a lineup of deeply evil men with far too much power.

Then I run back to Declan's office . . .

Ravi is waiting in the coffee shop for me, at a table in the back, with an espresso and an assortment of pastries arranged in front of him. He's wearing his sunglasses, since the interior is drenched in the sunlight streaming through the window.

I toss the flash drive onto the table. He takes it and slips it into his pocket.

"Excellent work, Astrid," he says, then holds out his hand, palm up. "Please, help yourself to something. I fear I ordered too much, but I do have a bit of a sweet tooth."

"Do you know what that is?" I ask.

He nods his head, his face set in stone.

"What's going to happen?"

Ravi shrugs. "It ends."

I look around, to make extra sure there's no one in earshot. "And what about those men? What happens to them?"

"Did you look?"

"Of course I looked."

"You shouldn't have."

"What happens to them, Ravi?"

He responds by picking up a perfectly sculpted croissant and taking a bite.

"Which one of them paid to have him killed?"

"Immaterial," Ravi says. "He won't be hurting anyone else."

"And those men will just find a new source."

"We'll be addressing that," Ravi says. "Make sure they understand what we know, and that we have proof."

"So the cycle continues. What about the kids?"

"Your role in this is done, Astrid."

I look around the café. There's a man sitting in the corner; T-shirt and jeans, shaved head, cauliflower ears, and scarred knuckles. Backup.

"You didn't answer my question," I say. "What about the kids?"

"What about them?"

"Are you serious?"

Ravi takes another bite of the croissant and noisily swallows.

"We'll do what we can," he says.

Rage builds in my chest until it's practically another person sitting at the table with us, goading me to do something. To grab his trachea and yank, hard, tearing apart his windpipe, causing him to choke to death on his own blood. There's a butter knife on the table, for the croissant, and I could so easily drive it through the eye of the man he brought with him.

It would mean the end of my career, and then probably a visit from the Pale Horse.

It would end in my death.

But I don't want to die. That would be too easy. An escape from the punishment I deserve: living with the memory of what I did to Chea.

"I quit," I say.

"You don't quit this job."

I lean forward, keeping an eye on the man with the shaved head, who suddenly seems to be paying more attention to us. "You want to come after me, you can come after me. You'll regret it."

"I got your back twice now, Astrid. This is how you repay me . . ."

"This is a bridge too goddamn far," I tell him. "I want no part of you or this fucking Agency. And don't forget the things I know. The mechanisms I may have set up for those things to get out, in case something happens to me."

His mouth becomes a flat line.

I get up and walk out of the café, staring down the man in the corner.

Neither of them follow me, but I can't be sure I don't have a tail, so I spend the next hour walking, hopping into cabs, jumping out, taking the subway. As a white American woman I can't help but stand out, but I do my damned best to make sure that I throw any tails.

Finally I get to my intended location: a storage facility. I go inside and the man behind the counter smiles at me and says, "Ni hao."

"English?" I ask.

"Some," he says.

I ask him for a small locker, and he quotes me a price in yuan that works out to about twenty USD a month. I pay for the next five years and he gives me directions through the facility to my unit. I climb through the sterile space, the lockers all painted a lovely shade of blue, until I find the one I'm looking for. It asks me to key in a code, which will be my PIN. I pick the day and month of Chea's birthday, and when the door swings open, and I'm sure I'm alone, I place the other flash drive, the one I found in Declan's office, onto the cold metal surface, then close and lock the locker.

Better to get it off my person as soon as possible.

Until I decide what I want to do with it.

ASTRID

The Tenth Circle
Now

Consciousness flares up on me like a blaring alarm. I sit up on the bed, trying to make sense of what just happened. It takes me a moment to realize that Vogt is there, sitting in a folding chair across from me. The sight of him startles me; I'm used to being alone when I wake up.

"Good," he says.

"The hell is going on . . ." I try to say it, at least. The words are mush in my mouth.

"Astrid, I have some difficult news to share," he says. "It seems we have . . . reached the end of our time working together. It is a shame. I have learned so much about you!"

"But I . . ."

"You may be a little groggier than usual. I experimented with the compounds I have been giving you. It troubled me that you could hear me. It is my desire for you to feel no pain."

Usually I come out of these with some sense, some idea of what it was Vogt was digging for. But all I have now is an empty void. I have no idea which folder in the filing cabinet he was rifling through this time.

"At this point, we will move on to the brain stimulation." He looks around the room. "In an environment such as this, I will not be able to do anything if there are complications. I will do my best."

"Why are you telling me this?" I ask.

"Because," Vogt says, leaning forward, "I desire to further my research. And like it or not, Astrid, you are a killer. I am deeply sorry for the traumas you have suffered in your life. But it is no excuse for the way you have behaved."

"Wait, why are we done?" I ask. "Why now?"

Vogt simply smiles. "Because I have what I need."

He stands and places a bundle down on the chair.

"I have some business off island to attend to, but I will be back to collect you tomorrow," he says, and then he leaves, closing the door behind him carefully.

Sitting on the chair in his place is a blue jumpsuit.

It doesn't sit well with me, that he finally discovered this mysterious thing he needed, and I still have no idea what it is. But I take some comfort in knowing how much easier he just made my escape plan.

The change in wardrobe makes me feel like a fresh cut of meat. Before, the other inmates just skimmed over me. But stepping into the yard wearing blue is a whole different thing. Now I'm a free and easy target.

Domingo, at least, still looks friendly. He's in conversation with a man I don't know when his gaze drifts my way, and he does a double take. He exchanges a few more words with the man, pats him on the shoulder, and then moves my way.

I keep an eye on Yumei and her two friends—the three of them are conferring at the other end of the yard, probably planning how best to attack.

"I guess today is not your day," Domingo says.

"The pink definitely worked better for my skin tone, but this isn't so bad," I tell him.

He looks at something over my shoulder, and wraps his fingers around my triceps, leading me ten feet. I guess he knows where the microphones are out here. He leans into my ear, and barely above a whisper, says, "The silverware in the dining hall. They don't always know when it goes missing. Easy enough to sharpen. Just don't get caught with it."

"Thanks," I tell him, trying to speak softly. "Not in the market for that kind of thing at the moment. What I really need is a cell phone."

One small piece of a much bigger plan.

He shakes his head. "Guards are spooked after what happened. Supply line is cut off. Anyway, I have yet to convince someone to stick an iPhone in their ass. The shape . . ."

I check on Yumei and her friends, still talking while staring at me.

Good. Let them come.

"How about this," I say. "What if I wanted to ask all the inmates a question. I need them to opt in to something. And I can only do it if everyone agrees. Could you facilitate that?"

He glances around the yard, then nods.

I get close to his ear and whisper the plan. As I do, his lips curl into a smile.

"I can make that work," he says.

"Good," I tell him. "But that last part is important. No one dies."

He shrugs. "Can't make any promises."

"Do your best, then."

"What about . . ."

But before he can finish his thought, a whipping sound rises over our heads, and we catch a brief glimpse of the helicopter as it floats into the sky and disappears. Vogt, on his way back to the mainland. Which means, on cue, the crowd moves toward the center of the yard.

Good.

Another part of the plan.

Before anyone has a chance to step into the circle of cheering prisoners, I dash to the center of the ring and yell, "Yumei!"

The crowd parts, and she steps in. She's still in pink, and I think the implication here is clear: they know we have beef, and Yumei can kill me for all anyone cares. I'm expendable now. Her two friends wait on the sidelines. I imagine if I get the upper hand, they'll come out to help her.

This is not how I had hoped to make my amends to her, but it's the best I got.

I stalk forward until we're almost nose to nose, and I speak to her only as loudly as it takes for her to hear me. "I want to say something to you. After I'm done you can do whatever you want. You can beat me to death. I don't care. Okay?"

She shifts back slightly and swings a wide punch at me. She may as well have explained it to me first. I catch it and hold it tight, her hand hovering near my head.

"Once I'm done, I won't fight back," I tell her. "But until then, we have to make this look good."

And I smack her clean across the face, just hard enough to stagger her.

She turns, furious, and tackles me, knocking us both to the ground. We roll around a bit, my mouth and eyes filling with kicked-up dust, until I'm able to get her in a lock on the floor. I get close to her ear.

"I worked for an organization called the Agency. I was an assassin. But the CCP wanted you back. I did what I did because that was my job. I did what I was told."

I loosen my grip a little, and Yumei is able to wriggle away from me. She scrambles to her feet and throws a kick into my side. I catch it and twist her down until she's on top of me. I put her in a guillotine hold, locking my arms around her neck and smothering her with my body, so I can be close to her, trying to block out the sounds of the people screaming and cheering around us, which is, hopefully, blocking out the microphones.

"No matter what happened, you were going to end up where you did. I'm not asking you for forgiveness. But I thought you at least deserved an explanation."

Yumei stops struggling for a moment, then goes back to trying to break free.

"The reason I'm telling you this now," I say, "is because I think I can get us out of here. You have privileges in the medical wing. I promise to take you with me."

Her body seems to slacken a bit when I say that, like she's really and truly listening.

"I will do everything I can to protect you on the outside," I tell her. "I know people. I can set you up with a new identity. The CCP won't find you this time."

Chea's face conjures in my memory, and I hope I'm not making this girl a promise I can't keep.

Her two friends are moving toward us now, but Yumei catches sight of them and throws her hand back, gesturing for them to stay out of it.

"So what do you say?" I ask. "Want to get out of here?"

I loosen my grip enough for Yumei to break free and climb on top of me. She hammers her fist down into my face. Over and over. When I think that this whole thing has been lost from me, she pulls me by the collar and gets close to my ear.

"What's the plan?" she asks.

"Let's fight a little more," I say, "and I'll tell you."

We get up and trade blows, but it's more of a dance than a fight. I explain to her what she needs to do, and she nods as I go. When I'm done I ask, "Is that all doable?"

"I think so," she says.

"Good," I tell her. "The next shift change should be tomorrow. Now we can end this."

I step back and offer myself to her. She punches me hard in the stomach and I go down. Yumei puts her arms up, triumphant.

Quraishi comes to me, like I knew he would. He crouches down next to me, but I put my hand up to let him know I'm fine, then grab his shoulder and pull him close.

"Yumei is on board," I tell him. "Domingo, too, so we can get everyone out of here. Talk to him. Can you do that? Help him?"

"I can," Quraishi said. "And what are you going to do?"

"Tomorrow I'm going to kill Dr. Vogt."

Quraishi raises an eyebrow at me when I say this. "I thought . . ."

"Don't worry," I tell him, spitting blood into the dirt. "I have a plan."

VII

Adversity truly introduces us to ourselves.

—THE BIG BOOK OF AA

MARK

There's a gap in the wooden boards nailed across the window. I lean against them to peer through. Less because I need to get a better look at the surrounding area, and more because my body feels like I just spent three hours inside a dryer. Standing feels unreasonable.

At least this part was easy. The ride to Guarujá was uneventful. Enzo dropped us a few blocks from the shipping yard that Lavigne's contacts identified. It was well-protected, with high barbed-wire fences and security cameras and roving guards.

Well-protected against normal people, at least. It took us all of five minutes to find a weak point. Then we basically waltzed in, and found this building, a small warehouse probably used for storage, currently sitting empty. There are discarded pallets strewn about the space and an empty office in the back, and that's it.

Now we just need to find the helicopters.

Booker hands me a bottle of water. "You good?"

I take a swig, swallow, and it tastes metallic. I swish a little more in my mouth and spit, leaving a stream of pink on the concrete floor. "Fine," I tell him.

"So what's the plan?" Booker asks me. "Just gonna drop in, see how things go?"

"Prisons are designed to keep people from breaking out, not breaking in," I tell him. "Ideally we're going to pose as guards. The only problem is they're likely using local talent and none of us are going to pass for Portuguese. We'll have to play it by ear."

"Simple," Booker says, a hint of exasperation in his voice. "And when we get to the black site prison that's surrounded by poisonous snakes?"

I stretch my leg, reaching down to run my hand over the gaiter. They're stiff, but they feel sturdy.

"Hopefully we land on the roof and never touch the soil," I tell him. "Between the three of us, I think we can make this work."

"Are we prepared for what may happen?" Lavigne asks, appearing next to us.

He doesn't need to say it.

I was ready to take the loss against Balor. I'm still pretty thrilled I managed to get through that encounter intact. But there's a lot of road left to travel, and the chance that any one of us could make a wrong move. Hit someone hard enough, they fall back and crack their head on the pavement and die. Whether we had the intent to kill that person doesn't matter. We accepted the risks, and the potential outcomes.

"If anyone's going to lose themselves in this, it's going to be me," I tell him.

"We're in this," Booker says, then glances at Lavigne. "I'm in this, at least. Not putting this on you. You're still free to walk away."

Lavigne shakes his head. "We see this through."

"I'm not letting either of you compromise yourselves for this," I tell them.

"Don't be a hero, Mark," Booker says. "I'll keep saying it if I gotta keep saying it, family ain't blood . . ."

"Yeah, yeah, I know," I tell him.

"We cannot wait around here all day," Lavigne says, hoisting the bat onto his shoulder. "We should get going."

"Okay, then," I say, checking my gear. Once I know everything is situated, we move out.

We cut through the yard, sticking to the shadows, staying out of the eyes of the few cameras we come across. It doesn't take long to find a lot behind a huddle of buildings. There are two helicopters sitting idle, and an empty spot for one more. I don't know what kind they are exactly, I just know they're utility copters, which means they're outfitted to transport both goods and people.

"Can't believe you're making me do this," Booker says.

"Oh right, I forgot, nervous flier. It's all right, big guy, I'll hold your hand."

"Shut up."

"Ei!"

The voice cuts through the quiet space. We turn to find an older man coming toward us, his greasy hair tied back into a sloppy ponytail. He's wearing a gray jumpsuit stained with oil, wiping his hands with a rag.

"O que vôce está fazendo aqui," he says.

"I think he's asking what we're doing here," I whisper to Booker and Lavigne.

"Are you kidding me?" Booker asks. "You speak like two dozen languages. You don't know Portuguese?"

"I can speak nine fluently and understand another five," I tell him. "I never worked anything in Brazil."

"We should have picked up an English to Portuguese dictionary," Booker says.

We all stand there, staring at one another with no idea what to say. I consider taking out my phone, to see if I have an app that'll translate speech, but before I can reach for it, the man breaks off into a run.

"Shit," Lavigne says.

He goes straight after the man, and Booker heads to the left, so I take the right, and we weave through the yard, seeing who'll get to him first. There are pallets and barrels everywhere, some stacked so high you can't see over them, and just as I think I've lost then, the man pops around the corner with a massive wrench and swings it at my head.

I manage to duck just in time to keep him from cracking my skull in half, but I stumble and lose my footing, landing on my back. He doesn't stay to finish the job, just drops the wrench and goes, so I drag myself to my feet and run after him. The guy is quick for his age; I lose sight of him almost immediately.

"Got him," Booker yells from somewhere to my left.

Which is quickly followed by the sound of a crash.

"No, I don't," Booker says.

I reach the corner of a building and find Booker on the other side, his hands on his knees, panting.

"You've been skipping your cardio, haven't you?" I ask.

"He's fast, we just . . ."

Lavigne appears from behind a large pile of pallets, holding the man in front of him, the bat across the man's neck.

"Thanks for that," I tell him. "C'mon. Let's get inside somewhere. Someone is bound to have heard all that racket."

We look for the closest enclosed space: a nearby office attached to a garage. We drag him inside and shut the door behind us, then sit him down in a roller chair. Lavigne zip-ties his arms and legs. The man has fallen quiet, seemingly understanding his predicament.

"You should jump rope or something," I tell Booker.

"What? Why?" he asks, still a little short of breath.

"Just because we don't work anymore is no excuse for getting slow."

"I still lift . . ."

"Throw in some cardio," I tell him, then I gesture to the helicopters outside. "Do we need a key for those things, or what?"

Lavigne peeks outside. "No idea, but I still think—"

An alarm blares from somewhere in the facility. We turn to find the old man has rolled the chair over to a panel and used his head to depress a big red button.

"Someone definitely heard that racket," I say.

Booker moves to the side of the window, his back flush against the wall, then quickly peeks his head around to assess the situation outside while staying under cover. He raises an eyebrow at us. "We got bogeys."

"How many?" I ask.

"A dozen so far," he says. "Armed."

I go to the dingy window, staying low, and find the yard is filling up with angry-looking men—some in tactical gear, who I'm guessing are guards, and some dressed in jumpsuits or denim. Workers at the facility. They're carrying an assortment of weapons. Batons, wrenches, hammers, but one has a shotgun and another has an assault rifle.

"Yeah," I tell him. "A few."

ASTRID

Quraishi is sitting on the bleachers in the yard, nose buried in the same Rushdie book. It's a slim volume, so I wonder if he's taking his time, or reading it again.

I keep my voice low. The doctor is back, and we don't have the luxury of yelling and cheering to cover up our conversation. "Had a very positive talk with Yumei," I tell him.

"Unexpected," he says, without taking his eyes from the page.

"You had that little faith in me?"

"I had more faith in her anger."

We look out over the yard, at all the other prisoners milling about. Yumei isn't here. Hopefully she's accomplishing the tasks I assigned to her.

"How about your end?" I ask.

Working with Domingo, I mean.

"It's a lovely day, isn't it," he says.

Yes, he means.

Quraishi puts down the book and looks around the yard. Not all of the prisoners are out here, but most of them are.

"What if some of these people . . . belong here?" he asks.

"Everyone deserves a choice," I say. "This place strips them of that."

"Do you know where the word 'assassin' comes from?" he asks.

I think about it for a moment, but I don't. It feels silly that I don't, but then again, I didn't know where my weapons came from, either. I just knew how to use them.

"In the eleventh century," Quraishi says, "a small faction of Shiite Muslims broke away from the larger Shī'ite community. The Nizari Ismail'i. They took refuge in castles in Persia and Levant—what is now Syria and Iran. Over the course of two hundred years they waged a secret war, killing hundreds of Muslim and Christian leaders. The word 'assassin' is said to derive from what they were known as: the Al-Hashishin. But the interesting part . . ."

He folds his hands and takes a breath.

"The interesting thing is that this was a sort of mistranslation. The Arabic word 'hashishin' means 'users of hashish.' This was what they were called by their rivals, the implication being that they were driven by base and criminal desires. Much can be said and debated about the various politics at play during this period, and their role in them, but it was always fascinating to me that the term came from a place of derision, and then took on such a different meaning."

"Such as?"

"Some fear us. Others celebrate us." Quraishi meets my eyes and says, "There is nothing noble about killing."

"You don't need to convince me of that," I tell him. "Anyway, back to your point, I have a friend who likes to say that stories get bigger in the telling."

"Indeed they do. Regardless of the origin, the Order of Assassins was feared, renowned. My father, from whom I picked up the torch that I carried for so many years, told me that we were descended from them."

"Do you think that's true?" I ask.

Quraishi shrugs. "Just like the words we use, we all come from someplace. But it does not matter where we came from. It matters where we go." He sighs. "I wonder what my life would have been like, if not for the way my father conditioned me."

That's a question I've asked myself many times.

What my life could have looked like had I been born into a stable family, with a loving mother and father, who didn't sell me off to support a drug habit.

If not for all that, would I have ever taken a life?

The only thing I know for sure is that so many people would be alive. Chea included. She'd be alive, but suffering. I wouldn't have been there to save her.

"I wonder about the inevitability of these things," I tell Quraishi. "If this life is what we were destined for, all along."

Quraishi picks up the book carefully, almost reverently, and says, "Your organization. Is it accepting of new members?"

"There's a process," I tell him.

"I understand my reputation precedes me in all things . . ."

"It's not that. Someone infiltrated us. Tried to turn one of our own back to his old life."

I think about what Mark would say.

All it takes is a desire to change.

"You would go through the process, just like anyone else," I tell him. "But I believe you would be welcome to join us."

The next thing Quraishi says is through a thick sheen of sadness in his throat. "Despite the things I have done?"

"Because of the things you've done, and the desire to not do them anymore. That's the only thing that matters."

"Thank you, Astrid, I . . ."

He falls silent, dropping his head into his hands. I place my palm on his shoulder and give him a squeeze.

"The doctor is going to come to collect me soon," I tell him.

Quraishi looks up and smiles at me, his eyes wrapped in tears. "Then we shall be ready."

MARK

Booker racks the shotgun and looks at me with a grim twist of his lips. "Either we're cocky or we're rusty," he says.

"Probably a little of both," I tell him.

I turn to Lavigne, who hefts the bat onto his shoulder and shrugs. "This doesn't mean the odds are in their favor."

"Still cocky, then," I say. "Good attitude."

I scan the cluttered space for something that might be helpful. The office looks like a bomb hit it. Machine parts and paperwork everywhere. There are a few tanks in one corner that could be flammable, if not explosive—but that's out, too much of a chance of killing someone.

There's shouting outside in Portuguese as Booker and Lavigne root around. I can't make it out, nor does it matter. The tone implies the overall mood, which is: bad.

Lavigne says, "Here."

He holds up a subcompact handgun. The three of us look at it with a degree of both fear and reverence. For any one of the three of us, that alone would tip the odds and make this entire thing end with a few well-placed shots. And as it stands, it's pretty much useless.

Watch too many movies and you might get the idea that shooting out a kneecap is easy. It's not. Guns don't always shoot straight. People are moving targets. Adrenaline can mess with your motor reflexes, even when you're a professional. The frenzy of a firefight is big and unpredictable.

"I got an idea," Booker says, picking up a fire extinguisher. He doesn't need to explain it. We toss it out the door, bang bang, smoke grenade. There are windows on either side of the office. One man out each window and then the third, whoever fires the shot, goes through the main door. We take them head-on, and from both sides, and between the three of us, with the cover, it ought to be short work.

Lavigne offers me the gun and says, "You should do it."

"Why?" I ask.

"Because I know you're a good shot," he says, turning his head to show me the mottled scar where his ear used to be.

He hands me the gun. It's a .380 Taurus. Never fired one of these but I've heard they're pleasant to shoot. The metal feels alien and uncomfortable in my hand. I haven't fired a gun in a long time.

I take a deep breath. The problems I used to be able to solve with this.

Booker rolls the man in the chair behind a pile of car parts, to keep him safe from the gunfire. Then he and Lavigne post up at the windows, both of them waiting for my cue. I crack the front door of the office open, then toss the fire extinguisher out. It rolls about thirty feet, the people outside immediately yelling, but not knowing what it is. I send one bullet into the side of it, and it explodes into a white mist.

Then we get to work.

I lose sight of Booker and Lavigne. Bullets cut the air, so I stay low. I approach the shape of a person, and as I get close, I unload a pepper spray blast into his face. He goes down choking. Another person appears to my right; I snap out the friction baton and send it into his knee. It breaks, probably—I think I hear the snap over the mayhem—but he'll live.

Something smashes into my back and sends me sprawling forward. I attempt to move with the momentum, combat roll to my feet, but I trip over the guy I hit with the pepper spray. I manage to get myself turned around just in time to see a tall man with an acne-scarred face standing over me, pointing the business end of a shotgun directly at me.

He mutters something in Portuguese, and I repeat the serenity prayer in my head.

Grant me the serenity to accept the things I cannot change, the courage to change the things I can, and the wisdom to know the difference.

But before he can fire, his face twists in pain and his body folds back. Lavigne drove his bat into the back of the man's knees, and he relieves him of the shotgun as he goes down. He delivers the heel of his boot into the man's forehead. Not enough to kill him, but more than enough to stun him.

Lavigne offers me his hand.

"We friends now?" I ask.

He doesn't say anything to that.

Booker comes ambling toward us, hoisting his own nonle-thal shotgun over his shoulder. The smoke is dissipating now, and the yard is littered with writhing bodies. Nobody dead, it seems. Lavigne hands us each some zip-ties and we make our way around, lashing hands and feet, so no one gets the bright idea to warn the prison, or take another run at us. I mutter apologies as I do so, but I don't think anyone understands them.

Once that's done the three of us return to the front door of the office.

"Now"—I gesture toward the helicopters—"who's flying this thing?"

"Not me," Booker says.

"I don't know how," Lavigne says.

"Well . . . shit."

I don't know how to fly it, either.

It starts small in my chest, and then explodes out, filling the space: laughter. Booker and Lavigne join in, and the three of us laugh our heads off like the idiots we are. Three expert assassins who aren't smart enough to figure out the most im-portant part of the plan. I want to say we have an excuse. There's a lot going on right now.

"We're a bunch of dopes," I tell them.

"Agreed," Booker says, still chuckling, wiping a tear from his eye.

Lavigne sweeps his hands around the men we subdued. "Perhaps we can conscript one of them? Or the man in the office?"

"That sounds like a good bet," I tell them, leading them back inside. The man is still alive, which is great, but he's not in a fantastic state. He's breathing fast, eyes wide, and when he sees me, he struggles against his restraints, like I might be there to finish the job.

I point back to the helicopters. "Can you fly those?"

He looks at me like I have six heads. "Fly," I say, a little louder.

"Speaking louder isn't going to make him understand you," Booker says from the doorway.

I put my arms out and pretend like I'm an airplane, making a whooshing sound.

"Moron," Booker says.

But the man nods. "Voar. Sim."

I turn to Booker. "Who's the moron now?"

"Still you," he says.

I pick up the gun and hold it on the man. I hate having to do it, but I need him to do what we tell him. We untie him and lead him over to the helicopter, where he climbs aboard, and we get on, too. There are headsets, so we put them on, and within a few minutes, the rotors are spinning and my stomach lurches as we climb into the air, then we bank hard as we head out to sea.

Booker's hands are gripped tight on the jump seat.

"You good, man?" I ask him.

He doesn't hear me. I fiddle with the controls on the helmet a little until I manage to turn on the radio. He sees me and does the same. I ask it again.

"I will be once we make it to the island," he says.

"Great."

We ride in silence a little, as I keep one eye on the pilot, to make sure he doesn't try to radio ahead. I don't know how long this is going to take, but the island is only twenty miles out. That can't be too long. I turn to Lavigne and tell him, "I think you're right. I think the way we punish ourselves is the worst part."

He stares at me for a few moments, long enough I wonder if his mic is turned on, when he asks, "Why did you stop?"

I consider making a joke—that is my strong suit—but figure part of this process is being honest, and if there's anyone I owe honesty to, it's Lavigne.

"I met a woman," I tell him. "Fell in love, considered leaving the game. You know how that story goes. Then her brother came into the house in the middle of the night to drop off Christmas presents. I thought he was there for me and I killed him. She was pregnant. My son is three now. I'll never meet him. That was my rock bottom."

Lavigne says nothing, but he holds eye contact with me, and for the first time, I think he sees me as a person, rather than as the main villain of his life story.

Booker looks back and forth between us but doesn't say anything, either. I haven't told him about the ear. And I don't want to. I don't know how he's going to react. Probably he'll try to talk us out of it, but I've made up my mind. If this is the price I have to pay, I will pay it gladly. No questions. I just hope Lavigne is willing to cut it off for me because I don't want to have to do it myself.

Booker looks about to say something when the pilot's voice comes in over the radio to break the tension.

"Você só vai me matar."

"What did he say?" I ask.

"Vou me arriscar com as cobras," he says.

"The hell . . ." Booker asks.

But before he can finish the sentence, the helicopter banks, hard, and we hurtle toward the water, my stomach doing flips. I catch a glimpse of land, then ocean, and then there's screaming, and the helicopter hits in a massive groaning of metal and a gush of water in my face that chokes me as I'm jerked around the seat, the seatbelt barely holding me in place.

We flip and turn and twist, the fuselage screaming around us, pain rocketing through my body from every direction as I'm wrenched around in the seat.

Then we're stopped.

Did I pass out? I might have passed out for a second there. The only sound is a ringing in my ears and the gentle flow of water somewhere underneath me.

I check on Booker and Lavigne—we're sideways, and the two of them look like they're hanging against their seatbelts, too.

The open door is below us, churning ocean water filling up the interior. Despite the blood trickling from Lavigne's hairline, they're alive. My whole body feels put through a spin cycle, but I don't think anything is broken. I undo my belt and fall into the fuselage, then crawl over to the front, but the pilot is already gone, his seatbelt dangling and swaying.

Shit.

If I had to guess, he decided to take his chances with the snakes.

I turn to find Booker helping Lavigne out, and then the three of us do our best to dig out our bags. We find some of them. It's sunset, and we have to wade about a hundred yards through waist-deep water until we find a smattering of rocks near the shore. We find a safe place to stand, and Booker takes out a flashlight and rips open the bags we managed to find. We still have some of the pepper spray blasters, but the shotgun is gone. Lavigne still has his bat.

The three of us look at one another, beaten and battered, and we all just let out a collective sigh. What is there to say, at a moment like this?

Other than, *It's been a day.*

"Shit," Booker says, and he dives into the bag, pulling out the case with the antivenom.

Both injectors are smashed, the contents dripping around the bag.

"Well," he says, tossing it into the surf. "There's that."

The three of us turn toward the island and make our way to the shore, careful not to slip on the rocks. In the distance, maybe a half a mile, through a dense clutch of trees, is a concrete box sticking out over the foliage.

That's where we're going.

Surely, at this point, they know we're coming.

So do the snakes, probably.

"Be careful where you step," I tell them.

ASTRID

When the knock comes at the door of my cell, I work on my box breathing, the way Mark taught me.

It's supposed to calm you down, lower your anxiety.

It doesn't help all that much.

Not with what I have planned next.

The door opens and Vogt pops his head in, smiling like he's picking me up for a date. "Are you ready?"

"Do I have a choice?" I ask.

"Sadly, you do not," he says, the smile barely wavering.

I get up and look around the cell. It felt like a safe space, as safe as something can feel in a place like this. I step out into the main room and catch Quraishi and Yumei sitting at a table together. Not close to each other, but close enough I feel at least somewhat encouraged. Domingo is standing on the other side of the room and gives me a slight nod.

Game on.

"This is the first time you will be coming to this area awake," Vogt says, like it's a mildly interesting fact.

"Yeah, cool," I tell him.

Mark would have said something funny.

But I'm not Mark.

And I wonder if he would approve of this.

But the more I think about it, the more I know it's the only option.

There are four owls with us now, all of them with stun sticks. Vogt isn't stupid; he has to figure I'm not going to go through with this quietly.

And I'm not.

We make it through a corridor to a set of double doors, where Vogt keys in a security code that he doesn't even bother to hide from me—2-3-5-9.

We step inside and it's like a completely different facility. The air is ten degrees cooler, dry and antiseptic. There's a low thrum making me think they have a separate HVAC system in here. Everything is neat, the metal surfaces gleaming, the rooms and hallway covered in blue tile. There are a series of doors on either side of a long hallway, and he leads me to one halfway down, which he opens and beckons me to enter.

It's a surgical suite, full of expensive equipment, beeping and blinking away. At the center of the room is a chair with a three-point craniometry headrest. A brace where I'll be seated, and kept still, while Vogt drills holes into my skull, cuts off the top of my head, and digs wires into my brain.

"Please," Vogt says, like he's escorting me to a seat in a fine restaurant, "be seated. Get comfortable. It's going to take a little while."

He turns his back to me as the owls clamp my hands and feet to the chair. The restraints are heavy, made of thick leather.

Which is fine. I planned for this, too.

Another owl enters, crosses to Vogt, and whispers something in his ear. Vogt says, "That wasn't scheduled. Contact the mainland and keep an eye on the exterior cameras. Otherwise I am not to be interrupted."

The owl leaves. That's interesting. But in this moment, not important. The only thing that matters is whether Yumei came through. I watch the four remaining guards. The new shift arrived a little earlier today, which means they all should have been dosed with snake venom already. They look fine, standing ramrod straight. Vogt is carefully assembling a series of tools on a table in front of him. I can't see what he's doing, which makes it all the more terrifying.

"So at this point, you're just doing this for kicks?" I ask.

"No, Astrid, I'm doing this for science," he says. "This was part of my deal with your benefactor. That once we retrieved . . . what we needed to retrieve, I could do with you as I pleased. Over the course of the past week I've been dosing you with a variety of drugs, and using a variety of techniques to further my research in memory retrieval. I now seek to get a more clear picture of what's going on in that beautiful brain of yours. This will serve a dual purpose, of letting me directly examine how those medications affected you, but also allow me test this apparatus, so we may make use of it again in the future."

"What do you mean, part of the deal?"

He turns to me, holding a gleaming dissection saw.

"Given the scope of what I'm planning, you're unlikely to survive, so I suppose there's no harm in telling you now, is there?" he asks. "The cost of keeping people here is quite steep, and your benefactor did not have the funds necessary for this project. So we struck a deal. As long as I got her the information she required, I could use you to further my research. It was a unique arrangement, but she made a very compelling case."

"What you're doing to the people in here is wrong," I tell him, stalling for time.

"Think of how elegant all of this is," he says. "A human race that requires medicine, information, tools for survival. We've had this conversation, Astrid. While I do enjoy you as a person, make no mistake. You killed people. Those men you killed, did they not have families? Someone who loved them? And don't say you were doing your job."

"It's a little more complicated . . ."

"And what about Chea?" he asks, his eyebrow arched, and for the first time in my stay here, there's a dark look on his face. "That poor girl. Dead because of you."

I want to argue. That she would have been dead either way. That I gave her the chance. That the world is a cruel and crushing place, especially to women, but there's a part of me that will always carry that mistake. That if I had told her no, that I wouldn't train her, she might still be alive.

She was dead the moment I offered to take her in.

That's the truth.

The romanticism of the idea, extinguished by the cold breath of reality.

I tense my hands into fists. I want to smash every one of them into liquid. This thing inside me, this rage, I thought this stupid program was supposed to get me to set it aside. And I can't. It's here. It's always here.

Maybe I am hopeless . . .

"Gabriel, Bernardo, traga-os por favor," Vogt says.

Bring them in, please.

Two of the owls briefly step out, then return with Domingo and Quraishi, both of their faces bruised and bloodied. Their captors kick them behind their knees so they fall down into a kneeling position.

"Before we get started I did want to clear one thing up," Vogt says. "We caught wind of your little plan. It seems that our friend Domingo was warning the other prisoners that something was going to happen. I believe both of them are involved. They've withheld the details, but, Astrid, based on our analysis of the recordings here, I assume you are involved, too."

"I think you got your wires crossed," I tell him. "We were talking about starting a book club."

Just a little longer . . .

"Quraishi is still valuable for the things he knows, but Azevedo is no fan of your friend Domingo," Vogt says. "Which leaves us in an awkward position. Because while in most instances I do prefer to use noninvasive techniques to extract information, it seems at this moment, time is of the essence. So I will make you a deal, Astrid. Tell me what your plan is, and I will not order these men to stomp Domingo to death in front of you."

One of the guards throws Domingo onto the floor and presses a boot into his back.

"Thought you didn't like torturing people, asshole," I tell him.

Vogt smiles. "Well, I'm not torturing *you*."

Domingo is writhing on the floor and now I'm getting worried. That Yumei dropped the ball, that the dosage was wrong, that it's not going to work . . .

But then, one of the guards starts to sway.

There it is.

The other three join, almost in unison. Vogt doesn't notice until the four of them tumble to the floor in a heap.

Before he's fully turned around Quraishi closes the distance between them and throws his knee into the doctor's back. Domingo scrambles to me and works on unfastening the clamps.

Vogt freezes, unsure what to do now that the power balance is shifted. All that Sturm und Drang evaporated the moment he wasn't in control anymore.

As soon as I'm free I tell Quraishi and Domingo to go. Then I get behind Vogt and hook my arm around his throat, cutting off the oxygen supply to his brain.

"You don't have long, so I'll be quick, since you've been so straight with me," I rasp in his ear. "You've been dosing the guards with snake venom. Mithridatism, right? Yumei mixed some propofol into today's doses. They'll sleep for a bit, then they'll wake up and they'll be fine."

I increase the pressure, and Vogt struggles to breath.

"Getting Quraishi and Domingo in here was part of the

plan. I figured I would be restrained and would need someone to let me out. So as soon as you took me, they started talking about their escape plan, with my name in the mix, but in vague enough terms that you'd have to drag them in here and question them alongside me."

I set my grip, pulling back, practically lifting him off the floor.

"The only way we were ever going to get out of here was to cause a little chaos. You shouldn't brag about the Medusa Protocol. You thought you were scaring us, but really, you were giving me a way out of here. Because if you're opening the prison to the snakes, that means you're opening the prison."

Vogt's pulse slows.

"I will not die here," I tell him. "And I will not let you decide my fate for me."

Vogt's body goes rigid, as he makes one dying gasp for life.

Then he collapses in my arms.

I hold for another few seconds, just to be sure he's not faking.

His body slumps to the floor.

I check his pulse, and he's dead.

MARK

We make our way slowly over the rocks and uneven terrain, toward the prison wall in the distance. I'm practically holding my breath, hoping that I hear the snakes before I see them, which I'm sure is unlikely.

The sun is setting, but on the other side of the island. There's just enough light in the pink-to-purple sky that my eyes can't properly adjust.

The timing of this sucks.

"You asked about hell?" Lavigne whispers to me. "This is hell."

"Yo, snakes are attracted to sound," Booker says.

"You a herpetologist now?" I ask.

"No, but remember that episode of *The Simpsons,* where Lisa used stereo speakers to attract the snakes?"

"Okay, you are not a herpetologist. We don't make scientific decisions based on a twenty-year-old cartoon."

"I'm just saying, not going to hurt anything to be quiet, is all," Booker says. "We don't know what other kinds of security this place has."

Something flashes on the edge of my vision, between a pile of rocks. A snake, or is it my eyes playing tricks in the dwindling light? Who knows, could be both. I focus on my breathing, careful about where I take my next step.

"So what's the beef between you two?" Booker asks.

"Thought we were supposed to be quiet," I say.

"I know you two have history, and I respected the fact that neither of you seemed particularly forthcoming, but at this point, if we're going to die, I'd like to know," he says.

I don't say anything. It's Lavigne's story, if he wants to tell it.

"Mark took my ear," he says.

Booker turns and gives me a look. I want to offer a shrug—that's the only response I can think of in this moment—but it feels a little too pat. "I made my amends."

"Not yet, you haven't," Lavigne says. "In return for my help, Mark is going to give me one of his."

Booker stops and looks at him. "Dude."

"It is a fair price to pay," Lavigne says, his voice flat in a way that makes me think he is not going to reconsider.

"It doesn't feel in step with"—Booker waves his hand around—"the life we're trying to build for ourselves."

"I did not ask for his life," Lavigne said. "I asked him to understand the pain I live with every day."

"And I agreed," Mark said. "This isn't something we need to unpack. It is what it is. Now let's stop talking and go get Astrid, okay?"

Booker just shakes his head.

"Both of you, lunatics," he says.

"Right, because you're a bastion of mental health," I tell him.

He stops. The muscles in his back tense.

That was a low blow. All of us are haunted by the ghosts of the people we've killed. Booker more than the rest of us. He literally sees them. His doctor says it's a PTSD thing. The more he talks about it—the way they appear in his bedroom at night, or follow him around in the grocery store, or hover outside the window of his living room—the more I think there might be something to it.

That's why he doesn't sleep.

He unpacks that, every week.

"That was a messed-up thing for me to say, Book," I tell him. "I'm sorry."

He nods without looking at me, and we continue on our way.

HALTing. Not hungry, not really. Angry maybe. Lonely, no.

But tired? Yes. Very. I took a beating and then was inside a helicopter that crashed. I'm not at my best in this moment. It's a wonder I'm still on my feet.

We make it over the rocks to a small jungled area. The canopy is thick, blocking the light, but the path through looks relatively clear, and beyond that I can just make out the outer wall of the prison.

"These things hang out in trees?" Booker asks.

"It said that on the Wikipedia page, yeah," I tell him. "They feed on migratory birds."

We take a quick survey of the area. There's an incline to the left of us. Steep enough we'd have to climb with our hands in the rock outcroppings, which clearly is not an option. To the right is a forty-foot drop to a rocky shore.

"You know what they say," I tell them. "The only way out is through."

Booker mutters something under his breath, and we step into the darkened foliage. We make it ten feet in before something *thumps* to the ground behind us, and I nearly shriek, which is not very befitting of the world's deadliest assassin, even if he's reformed.

"Guys, I . . ." Booker starts.

And then he yells out, bending over at the waist, before throwing something away from him, into the brush. I dash to his side and he's cradling his arm, his face twisted in anguish. As I'm thinking of the best way to help, something heavy lands on my shoulder, and something sharp digs into my collarbone.

It rips free, Lavigne hurling a thick yellow snake into the trees. I reach up and press my neck, feeling the blood seep between the fresh puncture wounds.

"Well, this sucks," I say.

ASTRID

I scramble for the chair, searching underneath it, hoping that Yumei came through for me. Because I will not be what Vogt thinks I am. I will be better than that. I *am* better than that.

Quraishi comes into the room, kneels next to Vogt, and checks the man's pulse.

"He's gone," Quraishi says.

"Domingo?"

"The guards are all down. The prisoners have assumed control. Thus far it is peaceful."

"Good," I say, still searching, and . . .

There.

I pull the syringe out and check it. Full and primed. "How long is this supposed to take to kick in?" I ask. "The Medusa Protocol."

"I don't know. How long can we leave him like this?"

"Three minutes, tops."

We freeze in the silence. I listen harder than I ever have before, hoping that something will happen to let us know the protocol has been tripped. Muffled shouts drift our way, but that's it. No alarms. No bells.

"Astrid, if this doesn't work . . ." Quraishi starts.

"I know," I tell him, holding the needle.

Seconds pass. I keep an eye on the clock on the wall to confirm they are, in fact, seconds, and not eternities.

One minute.

Vogt's brain is dying, starved of oxygen. Too much longer and this won't work . . .

An alarm sounds somewhere deep inside the building, in tandem with another noise, a slight rumble in the ground below us.

"Good enough," I say, and I grasp the needle in my fist, pushing it hard through his sternum, and into his heart. I depress the plunger, pull it out, toss it into the corner, and start chest compressions as I hum the tune to the Bee Gees' "Stayin' Alive" in my head, trying to keep pace with the beat of the song.

Vogt's body jolts from the movement.

"Should we use a defibrillator?" Quraishi asks.

"Movie bullshit," I say, breathing hard. "Defibrillator shocks an abnormal rhythm back to normal. Doesn't bring back one that isn't beating."

"Astrid, we should move," Quraishi says. "Domingo is on the way to contact his people, to get transport out for the prisoners and the guards. I don't know how long we'll be safe . . ."

"Leave me," I say, breathing hard, continuing the chest

compressions. "Move everyone to the cafeteria. Try to keep this contained, in case the snakes start getting in."

"Astrid . . ."

Vogt still isn't moving. I press his chest harder, trying to jump-start his heart. Trying to crack his ribs. Trying to force his life back into him. Praying. I knew this was a risk, a big one, and I convinced myself I could pull it off.

It's not as simple as going back to counting days. Because then, what's the point of this? I can just kill whoever I want as long as I restart?

It means I haven't changed; I've just created a system of excuses.

And I *want* to change.

"Astrid," Quraishi says, putting his hand on my shoulder.

I shrug it off and keep pumping, Vogt's face blurring in my vision. I choke back a desperate sob.

It's not his life I'm trying to save.

It's mine.

Vogt arches his back, gasps, and coughs, his face purple but slowly softening to red. He sputters and tries to speak, and for the first time, a feeling I can truly describe as serenity washes over me.

You were wrong about me, I want to tell him.

Even I was wrong about me.

"Welcome back, Doc," I say.

"What . . . happ . . . ed . . ."

The alarm stops ringing, disappearing along with the shuddering earth.

"You were dead for about two minutes. Long enough to

trip the protocol. Lucky for you, I was a field medic. A dose of adrenaline and some CPR got your heart started again. Though I suppose it didn't feel nice, did it?"

Vogt coughs in response, sucking long, desperate breaths into his lungs.

"Now tell me," I say, leaning close to him, "who put me in here, and what were they looking for?"

I put my mouth right next to his ear.

And he tells me.

I fall back against the cold tile. It's like when you try to remember a dream, and it's just beyond your grasp, and it comes flooding back. All those memories he excavated. The worstest hits of my life.

"Where's the boat?" I ask.

"Back of . . . kitchen . . . door," he says.

There's something he's not telling me, his eyes darting quickly downward, his hand fluttering. Okay. There's a boat, but what's the use of having a boat if anyone could use it. There's a thin silver chain around his neck. I grab it and yank it off.

A key dangles from the end of it.

I'm going to assume this is the only copy. Vogt seems like the kind of person who would only be interested in saving himself.

I stand, consider smashing my shoe into his skull until I shatter it and then tracking the remains of his brain matter behind me through the prison. But it's not worth the effort. I want to save it. Every ounce of energy I have. I'll need it, for the task ahead.

"Astrid?" Quraishi asks. "Are you okay?"

"Fine," I tell him, the words flat coming out of my mouth. "I need to end this."

As I'm leaving, Quraishi puts his hand on my shoulder, but I shake it off. He calls something after me, but I don't hear it.

There's only one thing left to do.

Kill Madeline Mather.

Except her, I'm not bringing back.

MARK

A bite on my neck, this close to my heart, I should be in a terrible amount of pain—and maybe dead, not soon after. But it feels like a normal puncture wound, and I know puncture wounds. I have plenty of them. I'm not believing my luck just yet, but this might have been a dry bite.

Booker wasn't so lucky.

He's hunched over, groaning in pain, his arm angry and red around the bite mark. Every muscle in his body is tensed so hard I'm afraid he's going to tear something.

"What do we do?" Lavigne asks.

"We get to the prison," I tell him. "They must have antivenom there. Until then, we move fast but step carefully."

"I'm . . . fine . . ." Booker says through gritted teeth.

"Yeah, yeah, you're a tough guy, I get it," I say, hooking his good arm over my shoulders. I don't know if we should elevate the other one—probably not—and Lavigne seems to have the same idea, simply holding him around the biceps of his bitten arm as the three of us make our way through the jungle.

"So," I ask Lavigne, "you regret joining us for this little jaunt yet?"

"I regret a great many things," he says. "Helping a fellow will never be one of them."

"Wish that attitude extended toward me, but hey, whatever works," I say.

He seems to want to say something, but he doesn't. We walk a little longer, clearing the trees, and my breathing gets easier. Less of a chance of aerial snake bombardment. It's only another fifty yards to the prison wall, and the pathway is clear. It towers over us and it's a smooth surface, nothing to climb.

We walk along the edge until we find a door. There's a key-pad to access it. We prop Booker up against the wall. He holds his arm and groans, his head drenched in sweat.

Lavigne pulls a small device out of his pocket—a plastic gadget the size of a pager. I peek over his shoulder, and it has a yellow LCD screen with a rudimentary animation of a dolphin on it. The writing is Japanese.

"What the hell is that?" I ask.

"Got it at Enzo's," he says. "A digital multi-tool for hacking basic RFID and radio protocols. Should get through this, if I can figure it out."

"Do your magic, bud," I tell him.

As Lavigne clicks through the device, holding it near the keypad, I check on Booker. He looks at me with, for the first time, real fear in his eyes.

"Hurts . . ." he says. "Maybe . . . what I deserve . . ."

"Hey, we don't deserve to suffer," I say. "Yeah, we did some terrible things. And maybe in the end none of us are going to see heaven. But no one deserves to suffer. That's just perpetuating the cycle we're trying to break."

"It all ends in suffering, man," he says. "I know exactly where I'm going after this."

"C'mon, Book . . ."

"No, you may not believe in hell, but it's real. We all gotta go somewhere, okay? I earned my ticket. And they're all going to be waiting for me." He looks up, his eyes rimmed in tears. "That's what they're saying to me. They don't say it, but I know it. They're waiting for me."

I want to disagree with him. I want to tell him that hell isn't real, that it's a fairy tale concocted by the church to get you to give them money for shit. It's not even in the Bible. But I see the desperation gripping him right now, and there's nothing I can do to convince him otherwise.

"You stay with me, okay?" I tell him. "The meetings are going to be really boring if you're not there to give me shit."

He takes a deep breath, sighs, and dips to the ground.

"Just need to lie down . . ."

"Hey." I grab him under the arms, push him up, and slap him across the face, hard. "Stop that shit right now. You're not leaving me. You're my family. You hear that? What do you keep telling me? Family isn't blood . . ."

Booker nods. "I know, I know . . ."

"Now stop being such a baby."

Booker smirks. "Love you, too . . . you stupid . . ."

Before Booker can finish the thought, an alarm rings inside the building. But there's something else, too—an earthquake? But a subtle one.

The door clicks open, swinging ajar about a foot. Lavigne and I look at each other, wondering if we should be preparing for something to come through, but nothing happens.

"Huh," Lavigne says.

"After all the shit we've had to deal with today, maybe we got lucky?"

Lavigne turns toward the path behind us and says, "Rather the opposite, I think."

There are a dozen snakes crawling toward us. More are emerging from the jungle, heading our way. If the door popped open to allow it, that means whatever's going on inside can't be good. But it's not like we have another option, so we both grab Booker and hustle him inside, then close the door and manage to get it fastened before the snakes reach us.

We're inside a long corridor, the lighting so harsh it makes my skin buzz. There are two slumped bodies in black tactical gear, wearing white, featureless masks. We all stop, waiting for something to happen, and nothing does. I go to the closest body and check the man's pulse. It's slow, but it's there.

And then the alarm stops.

Lavigne helps me carry Booker as we make our way down the corridor, until we find another room, the door cracked open. We step inside to what looks like a medical suite, with some gnarly equipment. There are two older men on the floor. One is wearing a white lab coat and looks like a couple of miles of bad road, while the other, a Middle Eastern man with a gray beard, is kneeling over him.

"Antivenom," I say.

The man on his knees looks at me and shakes his head. Something about him strikes me as familiar, but I can't place it. He has a vaguely threatening aura about him, and he's wearing a pink jumpsuit, which means he's most likely a prisoner here, but he seems more concerned with the man on the floor. I can worry about him later.

I tear through the suite, checking the rooms, until finally I find one stocked with supplies. It doesn't take long to find injectors that look similar to the ones that Enzo gave us. The writing on the box is Portuguese, but there's a yellow sticker with a picture of a black snake on it.

I grab a few and head back to Booker, then jab one above the wound, and one below it. The skin is black around the edges of the bite. His face is a rictus of pain but as soon as I toss the spent injectors, he's softening.

"May I ask, who are you?"

I turn to find the bearded man, giving me a curious look.

"Mark," I tell him. "I'm here to rescue my friend. Astrid. Brunette." I hold up my hand, a little under my head. "Yea tall. Not super friendly?"

He nods. "I'm afraid she has gone."

"The hell do you mean, she's gone?"

"She told me she had to leave. Only moments before you came in. You must have just missed her."

"God damn it," I say. "Where is she going?"

"I'm not entirely sure," he says. "But the doctor may know.

He said something to her, about the person who was holding her here, and she left. She looked . . . angry."

I head back into the other room, where the doctor is sitting up against a cabinet, breathing heavily, holding his chest and grimacing.

"Where's Astrid?" I ask.

"She killed me . . ." he says.

"You don't look dead to me."

"He has a dead man's switch in his pacemaker," the other man says, at my shoulder again. "Only to be used in case the prison is lost. It opens everything. We'd never survive the snakes, or the swim to shore. Astrid choked him to death to trigger it, then revived him to turn if off."

"Jesus . . ." I mutter. "Hell of a gamble."

Astrid only would have done that if she was desperate. I lean down to the doctor and look him in the eye. "Tell me what you know, or I'm leaving you to the prisoners. I'm willing to bet good money they're not fans of yours."

The doctor nods. "Your friend was placed here by . . ." He grimaces again. "Madeline Mather. The wife of Declan Mather."

"Right," I say. "That asshole pedophile. What was this, a revenge thing, then?"

The doctor shakes his head. "No, I was tasked with extracting Declan's client list."

Astrid killed Declan. That much she told me once. Oleander to mimic a heart attack. After his death, rumors circulated that he was trafficking kids. And it was suspected his wife was involved, but the court proceedings ended in a mistrial; not enough evidence.

I thought it was interesting that she didn't end up on a hit list, too. But the implication of that is clear: she didn't know who the clients were. It was probably a way for the two of them to build a wall, to protect the identity of the men on the list.

So why would Madeline want the list?

I turn to the older man who seems so invested in these proceedings.

"Who are you, anyway?" I ask.

"My name is Fahad Quraishi."

Oh.

"You're the Shiqq."

He nods solemnly.

"I wondered if you were even real," I say.

I'll admit, I've got a bit of an ego. It's what got me to where I am in the first place. And people will often say I'm the best hitman in the world. And right now I feel like a Little League baseball player in the presence of Mickey Mantle.

"Astrid made mention of you," he says. "Mostly in passing. I did not know she meant the Pale Horse. I would like to help you."

"And why's that?" I ask.

"Because I believe we have a commonality in the things we are seeking."

"What is that, exactly?"

"Redemption."

I see it, clear as day. That look in his eyes. Carrying the weight of the things he did, wanting to put them down, and knowing he never can.

So, bearing it.

"Which way did she go?" I ask.

Quraishi kneels down to the doctor. "Where is the boat?"

"There is an exit," the doctor says, "at the back of the kitchen. A white door. It should have deadlocked after the protocol enacted. The cove is otherwise inaccessible." He grabs Quraishi's sleeve. "Take me with you. Please."

Quraishi stands, shaking the man's grip lose.

"No," he says. "You will remain amongst the people here. More boats will come. The rest of the prisoners may decide your fate."

"Please . . ."

Quraishi looks at me and says, "Let's go."

"Cold, but okay," I tell him. We go to the other room, where Lavigne is winding a white bandage around Booker's arm, the counter next to him littered with cleaning supplies.

Lavigne and Quraishi freeze when they see each other. They have a history. I wonder how much that history is going to mean in this moment. But then Lavigne nods, and Quraishi follows, a silent understanding passing between them.

"Fine, give *him* a pass," I say to Lavigne. Then I turn to Booker. "How you holding up there, champ?"

Booker holds out his arm and flexes it. "I been shot, and being bit hurt worse than being shot. This still isn't a picnic, but it's a little better."

"Good," he says. "Astrid is headed for a boat. We're getting out of here, double-time. Try to keep up." I turn to Quraishi. "You know the way?"

"Yes," he says.

He leads us out of the office, through a corridor, and into a large open room full of prisoners and passed-out guards. A young Brazilian man is dragging an unconscious guard to join a pile of others in the corner. He gently lays down the body, comes over, and grasps Quraishi's shoulders, then kisses him on both cheeks.

"I was able to make contact with land," the man says. "The boats will arrive soon. We will move everyone through the kitchen and into the cove. We just need to figure out how to open the door. But I just saw Astrid head that way. Maybe she's working on it."

"Wait, wait," I say. "We need to find a guy named Domingo."

The man perks up. "Present and accounted for."

"Good," I tell him. "Enzo says hi, and he can't wait to see you."

His face takes on a boyish smile. "My love . . ."

"Domingo, keep everyone alive until then," I tell him.

He nods and dashes off.

We hoof it behind Quraishi, through the dining area and into the kitchen. It's not hard to find the door the doctor was referring to. The one that was supposed to be deadlocked.

It's thrown to the side and looks ripped off the hinges.

I sprint through onto an enclosed walkway, to find another door standing ajar. When I make it to the end of the ramp there's a small cove, enclosed by rock. And off in the distance, I can just make out the lights of a boat, disappearing into the darkness.

VIII

You know what the true definition of hell is?

It's when you die, you get to meet the person

you could have been.

—Former UFC heavyweight

champion Frank Mir

MARK

Lower East Side, Manhattan
Six Months Ago

L et me get this straight," Astrid says, leaning over the table, her voice hushed but angry, her eyebrow deeply arched. "The Agency paid you two-fifty a head?"

I feel a little embarrassed to admit it, but it seems like she deserves the truth. "Yup. Anything that didn't involve wet-works was a hundred."

Astrid sits back. "Those assholes. I got fifty a head, twenty-five for intel missions."

"Jesus," I say. "You wouldn't think the pay gap extended to this kind of work . . ."

We both get quiet as Lulu approaches the table to freshen up our cups of coffee. Snow is gently brushing the window next to us, and otherwise the diner is empty, save an old man sitting in the back, doing a crossword puzzle. We don't techni-cally need to be quiet around Lulu—she owns the place, she knows who and what we are, and she deals weapons out of the basement.

But some conversations are best kept confidential.

"Hey, Lu, the coffee is good today," I say, nudging my mug. "You finally stop brewing it in the bathroom? Switch out the used-oil filters? What's your secret?"

She looks at me over her thick glasses, her red-to-gray hair frizzing out like she hasn't slept in a month—which, frankly, is her standard presentation. She stares at me for a moment longer than is comfortable, then says, "Hmm," and walks away.

"She's got a crush on me, I think," I tell Astrid.

Astrid doesn't laugh. "Seriously, though. What the hell?"

"Is that why you killed Ravi?"

She pauses, then picks up her coffee and takes a sip.

The snow is piling up outside. I suspect I'll be sleeping on Astrid's couch tonight. It's already almost ten P.M. and I don't want to make the ride back up to my cabin in the Adirondacks. This isn't the kind of weather to be riding five hours on a motorcycle and frankly it was stupid to ride it down here in the first place, but my car needs a new set of brakes and I haven't gotten around to replacing them.

Should be clear by morning. P. Kitty can fend for himself for the night.

We haven't discussed it but Astrid knows I'm probably staying. It feels good to stay. The mountains are lonely. Not so lonely that I'll try for her bed; Astrid and I slept together, just the once. When I became her sponsor, the chance of that happening again went out the window. It wouldn't be appropriate. Too much can get tangled up there.

And I think she gets that, even though sometimes it feels like there's a slight gravitational pull between us.

The silence is growing deafening, so I keep pushing. "Because you said the director ordered it. Our mysterious boss. Who, I sometimes wonder if he even exists, or if it was just Ravi the whole time, playing one of his mind games. When you killed him, there was something else there. Something bigger."

Astrid nods. "He had it coming."

"For what?"

Astrid sighs and sits back in her seat, looking at everything in the place but me.

"Ravi used people," she says finally. "He used us as weapons and was indifferent to the cost. He used people outside the game, and didn't care, as long as he got what he needed. And this right here"—she taps the Formica tabletop—"this pay-gap thing underscores that. Because I'm a woman, I'm worth less? I was just as good as you."

I smirk a little at that, and her eyes go dark.

"It's not a contest," I tell her. "But let me just say, I'm glad we never officially threw down. Even though you were hired to come after me . . ."

"Did I tell you that I had quit, like, a few months prior?"

"Really?" I ask. "You didn't mention that."

"I had. But Ravi needed someone he thought could actually give you a run. I needed the money, sure, but when I figured out it might put me on the path to Kozlov . . ."

"Speaking of, how did it feel when Kenji killed Kozlov? I know you had it out for him. You never told me why."

"What's with all the questions all of a sudden?"

"Because you never share at group," I say. "You have to start working that muscle. It's not a requirement, but I promise you, when you start doing it, it gets easier. It even starts to help."

"Kozlov killed someone close to me," she says.

"I'm sorry. Who?"

"Her name was Chea. She was my protégée. It was my fault. I made a bad decision. Doesn't matter. He's dead. That's what I wanted. But do you know what happened after?"

"What?" I ask.

She shrugs. "Nothing. Nothing changed. I was still angry. Still carrying all this pain. I've sat with this, and thought it over, again and again. That maybe if I was the one to kill him, not Kenji, it would have made a difference. But I don't think it would have."

"Probably not," I tell her. "That's the thing about revenge. Nothing changes after you get it."

She sighs, takes a long swig of coffee. "So, about that eighth step."

"The dreaded eighth step," I tell her.

"How does it work?"

I spin my mug on the table a few times, then I take out my notebook. It's small enough to fit in my pocket, and thin, but nearly full. I place it on the table between us. She doesn't reach for it.

"You write down a list of every person you need to make amends to," I tell her. "Then you go make them."

"I can't make amends to people I've killed, can I?"

"You can make amends to their family members. Their friends. Their colleagues. I try to track down one significant person, someone who will understand. It's not just people you killed—people you hurt, too."

"How the hell are any of us supposed to get through this process alive?" she asks.

"Carefully," I say.

"And how did you handle that?"

I shrug. "Used my words. I live with the reality that one day I might sit down to do an amends and end up staring down the barrel of a gun, and it'll be the last thing I see. Though I'd be less likely to do an amends to someone who was carrying. It's good to watch them a bit first. Do a threat assessment."

"Why not make all of these living amends, then?"

"The point of this is, it's not supposed to be easy."

Astrid nods. "It's supposed to hurt."

"It's not punishment. But if it didn't hurt, it would mean it's not working. If you feel genuine sorrow and regret for the things you did, that means you're healing. It means you're still human."

Astrid picks up the notebook and turns it over in her hands but doesn't open it. She drops it back on the table.

"This sucks," she says.

"Spoken like everyone about to start their eighth step." I point toward the ceiling. "Somewhere Kenji is watching this and getting a real kick out of it. I was incredibly difficult about the whole thing."

"Has it helped?"

"It has, yeah. We all need to sit with what we did. We can convince ourselves the people we killed all had it coming, but that's not the truth. They were troublesome, and we weren't always righteous. Sometimes what we did saved lives. But the only life that matters is the one we took, and the hurt we caused in the process."

"What if the other person was evil? I mean, well and truly evil?"

I sit back, chewing on that one. "I don't know that anyone is really and truly evil."

"Some people," Astrid says, her eyes boring into me, "are evil."

There's a lot in that statement, and I don't relish the thought of unpacking it. Not in this white-hot moment. So I tell her, "Sure. But this isn't about them. This is about you. It's about forgiving yourself."

She sighs. "Why?"

"Why," I say. A question she's asked me so many times. And it's my turn to look around the diner, searching for the words, some way to unfurl this big map in my heart and show her the journey that I'm on, but is there any way to do that? I don't know.

"How do I make that amends for Ravi?" she asks. "He's dead. I don't know if he had a family. And even if he did . . ."

I shrug. "You stick to the program. Best you can do."

"Best we can do," she says.

"And maybe at the next meeting, try sharing," I say. "I know it's hard, the first time. I mean, it wasn't that hard for me, I'm an external processor. But we're here for you, Astrid. We're your family."

"I had one of those once," she says. "They sucked."

"Well, we suck, too, just hopefully not as bad."

Astrid leans forward, like she wants to say something. Then she gets up and goes to the bathroom, and I sit there in the silence, thinking about all the dead people we've left in our wake.

IX

Nobody ever wins a fight.

—JAMES DALTON, *ROAD HOUSE*

MARK

Little Saint Sebastian, the Grenadines
Now

Lavigne guides the boat to the dock, and the four of us hop out, clambering across the wood. I glance back at Booker, and he seems to be okay; his arm is wrapped in a heavy layer of gauze and he probably doesn't have full use of it, but it's not like I was going to convince him not to come. Lavigne is locked and loaded, and while Quraishi is old, I still get goose bumps when I hold eye contact with him for too long.

A modern glass-and-stone mansion looms on the hillside above us. Little Saint Sebastian is a private island, once owned by Declan Mather, and now by his wife, Madeline. It's a wonder she hasn't sold it off. Declan was considered by many to be a billionaire, but it turned out a lot of his wealth was smoke and mirrors. He was cash poor and, as it turns out, asset poor, too, so this island is the only valuable thing they have left.

Though I guess the resale value of an island that was used to sex traffic children is not exactly high.

We've loaded up on nonlethals. Mather has to know she's in danger, so I'm sure she's called in reinforcements. Quraishi is the only one of us not carrying a weapon. We offered, and he waved it off, like they were children's toys. I don't know if that's because he's so far committed to where he is that he doesn't want to consider it—or if they really are just play-things to him.

Booker and Quraishi are lagging behind me and Lavigne, giving us a little space to talk. "So how are we going to do this?" I ask. "When we're done? You want my ear in a box, or . . ."

He doesn't respond.

"Could just do with a little direction here," I say.

"You are still willing to give it to me?" he asks.

"We made a deal," I tell him. "I'm not going to lie, I wouldn't be upset if you've reconsidered . . ."

He tosses me a glance. I'm not sure how to read his eyes. Maybe this whole experience has softened him a little.

"I have not," he says.

My stomach twists a little at the idea of cutting my own ear off. The skin on my left ear—I'll go with that one, if given a choice—prickles a little, but I ignore it. At this moment, it's not important.

As we reach a set of steps leading to the front of the house, there's a figure looming by the hedges, waiting for us.

Valencia.

She's wearing a leather jacket and black jeans, a nonlethal

pellet gun strapped to her hip. And she's got a look on her face that says, *What took you so long?*

"Are you kidding?" I ask. "How'd you know to meet us here?"

"Booker," she says.

"What about Lucia?" I ask.

"She's with Ms. Nguyen," she says. "Astrid is family. C'mon. I only just got here. I was making my way up when I heard your boat coming in." She cranes her neck to look at Lavigne and Quraishi. "I see we've got reinforcements."

"Introductions later," I say.

We climb the steps, which lead to another pathway, and then another set of steps. I guess we took the scenic route. As we get closer, I prepare myself for the fight ahead. I have to imagine we beat Astrid here. She had the prison jumpsuit on her back. The trip would be too long and arduous for the boat she took. Meanwhile, we got back to São Paulo and we were able to get Enzo to charter a private flight to a nearby island.

Maybe that's just me being hopeful.

As we reach the top of the staircase, my blood runs cold.

There are a dozen bodies scattered around a courtyard leading to the front door, crumpled over hedges and sprawled out on the stone pathways.

Blood, everywhere.

"Shit . . ." Booker says.

My heart twists in my chest. I know Astrid's recovery isn't my responsibility. I know I'm supposed to be able to let go. But it's hard to see all this and not feel like I failed.

Lavigne leans down to one of the bodies and presses his finger to the man's neck. He waits a beat and says, "Dead."

"So is this one," Quraishi says from where he's kneeling next to another body.

Booker shoots me a look.

He doesn't need to say it. Astrid was a field medic. She knows how to save a life. And she knows how to end one, brutally and efficiently.

A familiar voice groans from farther afield in the carnage. "Missed the party . . ."

Balor. I sort through the bodies until I find his. He's lying on his back. One hand is grasping his wrist. The other hand is lying about ten feet away. He's trying to put pressure on it, but between the amount that's pooled around him and the pallor of his skin, he doesn't have long.

"I see you've met Astrid," I tell him.

"That woman," he says, "was the devil."

Balor groans and scrunches his body at the waist. Quraishi leans next to him and pulls a knife off the man's hip, then slides it quickly into his throat, ending his life.

Quraishi looks at me and nods. "He was suffering. And beyond our help."

I want to argue, to tell him we should have tried to save him—but I don't know if that's true. I don't know what to believe anymore.

We push our way into the foyer, passing four more bodies. And two more in the kitchen. One of them is skewered through the neck by a kitchen knife, dug so deep into the wall that his body is suspended.

This is a lot, even for me.

A woman yells from somewhere deep in the house. We all break into a run, to the sliding glass door for the back patio.

The view is grand—a cloudless sky, the most beautiful azure blue, in contrast to the gentle lapping of the ocean, stretching off into the horizon.

And there's Astrid. Still in her blue prison jumpsuit, which is drenched in blood, soaked and clinging to her body. Before her kneels Madeline Mather. Tall, thin, wearing a yoga outfit, her black-graying hair twisted into a bun.

She's crying. Her face is bloodied.

Astrid is pressing a gun to her temple.

ASTRID

I hear them before I see them. They clomp through the house, their footfalls discordant drumbeats. Or maybe they're not like that, and it's just that every one of my senses is blazing, and I could hear a butterfly flapping its wings a mile away if I tried to listen for it.

Madeline's eyes dart toward the sound of the sliding glass door.

"Astrid. Do you want to put down the gun and talk about it?" Mark.

I keep my eyes locked on Madeline. Her surgically augmented body stuffed into a clingy purple yoga outfit that probably cost as much as my couch. Her big pleading eyes make her look like a small animal, one I want to crush under the heel of my boot, slowly, so I can hear her squeal as she dies.

"Please?" Mark asks.

Anyone else, I wouldn't move my eyes. It wouldn't be safe. Not holding someone at gunpoint this close. But Madeline is nothing. I turn to look.

Booker is here, with Valencia. So is Quraishi, along with another man whose ear is missing. And Mark, with that big dumb grin he always has. Standing at the front of this little cohort, his arms spread, like the saint he thinks he is.

Seeing them all gathered like this should bring me some degree of comfort.

It does not.

I return my focus to Madeline and press the gun to her head, eliciting a whimper from the back of her throat. "Is this an intervention?" I ask.

"It doesn't have to be," Mark says. "But you sure did kill a lot of people out there."

"I'll go back to counting days tomorrow. One more, and then I'm done."

"Or you could walk away. Otherwise it's always going to be one more. That's the thing about addiction . . ."

"Do you know who she is?" I say, cutting him off. "Do you know what she did?"

"I read the papers," Mark says. "And I think I put it together, but why don't you tell me what's going on?"

I drop my arm to the side, holding the gun against my hip. Madeline looks relieved. I don't like it, so I put my boot on her chest and push her to the ground. She cries and falls into a fetal position. Then I walk over to Mark, the thumb drive clasped in my fist.

Madeline's prize. The secret they were looking for in my

head. They figured I saw the client list and might remember some of them. What they found was more than they'd hoped for. And in my drug-induced state, I told them the location of the locker, and the code to open it.

Nose to nose, this is the first good look I get at Mark's face, which looks like hamburger meat.

"The hell happened to you?" I ask.

"I was in a helicopter crash and I got bit by a snake," he says. "Tell me what's going on."

I take a step back, pointing the gun in Madeline's direction. "She had me put in that prison because I'm the one who killed her husband. Declan Mather. I delivered his list of clients to Ravi."

Madeline is still curled into a ball, shaking now.

"And she wanted the client list, to, what, blackmail the people on it?" Mark asks.

"Not blackmail, no. Blackmail means someone will send someone like me to kill her. She'll suffer the same fate as her husband. This bitch wants to restart the business. She wanted to get back to trafficking children, but she didn't know who to sell them to. Now tell me, Mark, I killed her husband. Does she deserve an amends? Doesn't she deserve to die?"

"Maybe," Mark says, stepping forward. "Maybe she does. Do you have to be the one to do it?"

He reaches me and the gun moves in my grip. I look down to see that he's placed his hand gently on the barrel.

"Let's put down the . . ." he starts.

I smash my forehead into his nose. He staggers back. The others make a move toward us, but he puts his hand up.

"Don't fucking touch me, you privileged, self-righteous asshole," I tell him. "You don't know what it's like to be treated like a thing. You killed more people than any of us, and people act like you're a god. And, what, now the path to serenity is to sit around and talk about our feelings while we let the world burn down around us? How are we supposed to sleep at night, knowing we can do things that other people can't?"

He tries to respond, but before he can, I throw a push kick into his stomach. He hinges back to absorb the worst of it, but he still loses his balance and falls back onto his ass.

"The idea that we can be better is a joke, Mark," I tell him. "We are god's broken toys. He smashed us together and twisted us into what we are. The one kindness we can grant in the hellfire of this world is to say that no one else has to suffer."

"It doesn't have to . . ."

"Some people just need killing," I tell him, pointing the gun back toward Madeline. "If for nothing else, to make an example of them. Remind the rest of them how vulnerable they are. So, no more slogans. No more recovery bullshit, okay? Madeline dies. I'll carry that weight. Because that's all I ever do," I say, turning toward the ocean, raising my voice until I'm screaming, "I carry the fucking weight!"

"What if you don't have to, though?" Mark asks.

The words I've been holding in sear my throat on the way out.

"I know how it feels to be sold," I tell him.

Everything gets quiet, like the wind chose that moment to cease blowing. Even with the gun in my hand, this is the most naked I have ever felt. All of them looking at me, their gazes of hurt and pity and disbelief burning my skin.

Why I keep my head down in meetings. Why I never accept their invitations to share.

Because if I shared, I would have to tell the truth.

And if I told the truth, they would see me.

"My family," I tell him through the pain in my throat. "My *dad*. You have no right to tell me what I can and can't do with my pain. Because it's mine."

Mark's face drops. He tilts his head and exhales hard, then nods his head.

"I'd like to say something, Astrid," he says, his voice even and quiet. "And once I say it, I'll shut up. I promise."

I take a few steps back.

"That man, your father, he wasn't your family, Astrid." Mark gestures toward the others. "We're your family. You know that saying, blood is thicker than water? It's a misinterpretation. The full saying is: 'The blood of the covenant is thicker than the water of the womb.' It means the blood you choose is thicker than the blood you're born with. The point is, family isn't blood, it's who you bleed for."

The gun shakes in my hand, along with my jaw, as I fight to hold back tears.

"I'm your sponsor, Astrid," Mark says. "You sponsor someone to save yourself, not the other person. I know I can't tie my recovery up in yours. Those are separate things. So I'm not going to tell you what to do, other than to say, I support you. Whatever you choose to do next, I will continue to support you. We all will. No matter what."

He gets to his feet, grimacing as he does.

"We'll wait right here while you decide what to do," he says.

The others offer me silent nods of affirmation.

I search for a response, something I could say in this moment, and come up with nothing. Sometimes there are no words left. So I stalk back over to Madeline and press the gun to her head.

I want to ask her, *How could you?*

Instead I think back to that bedroom in Albuquerque.

The first life I took.

And the second.

Hearing that scream ring out behind me, and turning to find my mother, her hand over her mouth, frozen in fear at what she'd discovered. Her husband dead, her daughter holding the knife. I thought maybe she wasn't home, that maybe she finally got away.

That maybe she was out looking for me.

But she wasn't. And she did the worst thing she could have done in that moment. She didn't apologize, didn't hug me like I so desperately wanted. She pushed me aside and knelt over that bastard and cradled his head and asked me, *How could you?*

So I picked up my father's gun and pointed it at her face and I asked: *How could* you?

And then I shot her through the eye.

The rage in me was so big, it was like the moon passing in front of the sun—an eclipse casting the entire world into shadow. I haven't felt the sun on my face since, and I'm tired of living in the dark.

I drop the gun at Madeline's feet, then get close to her ear.

"You're as good as dead. If it's not me, then it's going to be someone like me, hired by one of the people on that list who wants to keep their secret. So I'm giving you a choice. More of a choice than you ever gave any of those kids. You get to take the easy way out, and I suggest you do."

She stops crying. Her face goes calm. I see that serenity, accepting the thing she cannot change. I get up and walk past the assembled group, through the kitchen. They follow behind me, and before we make it to the living room, a gunshot splits the ocean air, followed by the soft *thump* of a body falling to the ground.

I walk in a daze out to the dock, where we climb onto the waiting boat, and I find a corner and sit. Quraishi appears at my side and puts his hand on my shoulder.

"I never got a chance," he says, "to thank you."

"Life on the outside is going to be tough, so don't thank me yet."

"No, not for that," he says. "Thank you for trusting me."

He gives my shoulder a reassuring squeeze, then he and the man I don't know disappear below deck.

Booker and Valencia and Mark sit on the bench with me. Booker's arm is wrapped in gauze, blood weeping through the cotton.

"What happened?" I ask.

He holds up his arm. "I got bit, too. But a proper bite. Not like Mark. He got a little bitty bite."

"And you got beat up by a helicopter?" I ask.

"That," Mark says. "Balor, too."

"You kill him?"

"No, but you chopped off his hand up there."

It comes back to me now, the frenzy of descending on this place. I can't even recall it clearly. All I can see in my head is fog. Bodies and blood, arcing through the air.

"Yeah, I guess I did," I say, shuddering a little at the thought.

"Not only did Mark not kill Balor, he somehow talked Balor out of killing him," Booker says.

"Of course you did," I say, rolling my eyes.

Mark shrugs. "I am very charming."

I turn to Valencia. "Lucia?"

Valencia smiles. I'm not used to her smiling. She looks beautiful when she does, her face glowing and soft. "With Ms. Nguyen. They're safe. I'm excited for you to finally meet her."

Exhaustion rolls over me like a wave. I wonder when I last slept. I'm not sure, at this point. And all I want to do is go somewhere and curl into a ball and fall asleep and never wake up.

Because I thought that by giving Madeline a choice, and choosing myself in the process, I'd be able to put down this weight.

But it's still here.

I rub my hands together, the blood on them, the blood of all those people, dried and cracked, seeping into my skin. No matter how well I wash them later, it'll still be there.

X

We must have

the stubbornness to accept our

gladness in the ruthless

furnace of this world . . .

—"A Brief for the Defense,"

Jack Gilbert

ASTRID

Church of St. Jude, Manhattan
Two Months Later

Today is the day, I tell myself.

Breathe in for four, hold for four, out for four, empty lungs for four.

Then I smack the side of the new coffee maker.

It's one of those pod things. It looks like a rocket ship. And it doesn't want to turn on. It's plugged in, and the water reservoir is full. I inserted a plastic pod that, supposedly, tastes like French toast, but when I press the ON button, nothing happens.

Ms. Nguyen appears, as if the sound of me slapping the machine summoned her. She presses a button on the side. The ring around the ON button turns blue. She clicks that, and something inside the contraption makes a whirring sound. A thin stream of coffee trickles into the waiting mug.

"This is needlessly complicated," I tell her.

"Talk to Mark," she says. "He likes the flavors."

"And all that plastic. It's wasteful."

Ms. Nguyen shrugs. "They make reusable pods."

She steps away as I bring the mug to my lips. Too hot. I set it down to cool and turn to survey the space.

It feels strange, being someplace other than St. Dymphna's. We spent weeks looking for a new location, holding our meetings in Mark's apartment until we found this—the Church of St. Jude in Chelsea, another property the archdiocese was looking to unload. I guess Catholicism isn't really in these days.

The church has been vacant for a few years now, and we're still in the process of clearing it out. The basement air is so musty it feels thick on my tongue, and there's a pile of broken furniture in the far corner. Half the tile is missing, which is no great loss, because the pieces that remain are cheap stick-on squares the color of flu-season phlegm. The walls were bare white, but Mark and Booker are halfway through painting it robin's-egg blue, to mimic the color in our old meeting space.

Because blue is supposed to be calming.

It may not be nice, not yet, but it's ours, and the condition just meant Mark could get it at a steal. He's going to put in security measures, like at Dymphna's, but also create some living space, in case the next soul who comes in needs it.

People like Quraishi, who had to crash on my couch as Gaius assembled a new life for him. Which he did, along with releasing Declan's client list to several news organizations. That's been fun to watch. No one's been arrested yet, but the vice president resigned, and a lot of the people on the list have gone into hiding.

Quraishi seems to be settling well into his new life. He was a ghost, so it's not like anyone is going to recognize him. He catches my eye from the circle of chairs, where he's sitting with Ms. Nguyen. Then he gets up and moves over to stand with me next to the new coffee maker.

"I heard from Yumei," he said.

"How's she doing?"

"Settled in Denver under a new identity. It seems she is safe, for now. She had a message for you."

I laugh. "Oh yeah? How many four-letter words did it contain?"

"She said you're still not even, but also, to say thank you."

That feels good, at least.

Quraishi leans back and looks around the space. "So, this is new. I heard about what happened to the last church. It was named for St. Dymphna, patron saint of the mentally ill. This one is St. Jude, correct?"

"Patron saint of lost causes," I tell him.

"Ah," Quraishi says, putting a finger in the air to make a point. "But we are not lost anymore, are we?"

"No," I tell him. "No, we are not."

He pats me on the shoulder and returns to the seat next to Ms. Nguyen.

Booker is huddled with Valencia. He has Lucia cradled in one arm, using his free hand to give her a bottle. His forearm bears a nasty scar, still in the process of healing, from where the snake venom ate away at his flesh.

But he's on the mend. So is Mark. The wounds on his face have knitted back together. The mottled mess on the side of his head, where his left ear used to be, is almost healed.

When I asked him about it, he said, "Family is who you bleed for," and he refused to elaborate any further.

Mark appears out of the back room, dragging two more folding chairs. One for him, and one that will remain empty for Kenji. He places them down to complete the circle and sits, giving me an expectant look. I pick up my mug and take a seat between Quraishi and Booker. The coffee is cooler and I take a sip; it tastes like cinnamon, not like French toast, but still, it is pretty good.

"Hey," Booker says, leaning over to me. "Want to take over?"

I give a look to Valencia and she smiles. "Go ahead."

I place my mug on the ground at my feet and Booker passes me Lucia, like he's handling an unstable nuclear device. As he deposits her in my arms, he makes sure the bottle stays connected to her lips, and then lets me take control of it. Lucia keeps drinking, content, her eyes closed.

She is so tiny, and so beautiful.

I know in that moment that I will always remain committed to my sobriety—but I will do whatever it takes to protect this girl.

"We ready?" Mark asks.

"Yeah," I tell him.

Mark reads through the opening script, and we take a moment of silence for fallen comrades.

"Valencia," he asks, "could you read the steps?"

She recites them, and we all laugh about not being saints, because that will never not be funny. With the front matter done and out of the way, Mark asks, "So, who wants to go first?"

I caress the top of Lucia's head with the hand that's cradling her and say, "I would."

Everyone stops. A collective intake of breath.

"Astrid," he says, beaming. "We would love that."

"My name is Astrid," I say. "And it's been two months since I killed someone. I guess it would make sense to start at the beginning. But I want to start by telling you about someone I loved, very much. Her name was Chea . . ."

I had hoped, as we drifted away from that dock in the Grenadines, that I could leave the weight of my rage behind. It didn't work out like that.

Then sharing, I thought, might be the moment when it would happen.

It's still here.

But the more I talk, the more I realize: it is a part of me, and it always will be. I don't need to put it down. I don't need to let it go or pretend that none of it happened. I don't need to force it inward and use it as a tool to punish myself.

I just need to greet it with care. I need to recognize it for what it is: the thing that made me who I am. Someone who is trying, today, to be a little better than I was yesterday.

ACKNOWLEDGMENTS

Thank you to everyone who supported me through this process: my friends in recovery, who I will not name for obvious reasons, but were kind enough to share their stories with me. If you're reading this and you think AA is something you might want to explore, visit www.aa.org.

To Todd Robinson, not just for his ability to take a stray idea I have and amp it up to 100, but for his generosity in doing so. Also: Alex Segura, Shawn Cosby, Eryk Pruitt, Mia Gentile, Cyn Grace Sylvie, and all my friends who egged me on.

And big thanks to Robert Zappalorti for teaching me stuff about snakes.

Thank you to my editor, Daphne Durham, for her incredible insights, and the entire team at Putnam, including Aranya Jain, Katie Grinch, and Molly Pieper. Huge thanks to Tal Goretsky, for the incredible covers he's created for this series.

ACKNOWLEDGMENTS

And thank you, as always, to my agent, Josh Getzler, his incredible assistant, Jillian Schelzi, and the entire team at HG Literary, as well as my film agent, Lucy Stille, and Lauren Abrahams and the team at Amblin, for their efforts to, hopefully, one day bring this to the screen.

Most of all, thank you to my daughter, Abby. One day I'll write a book you can read. But these are for you, too.

Rob Hart is the author of *Assassins Anonymous, The Paradox Hotel, The Warehouse,* and the Ash McKenna crime series, as well as the coauthor of *Scott Free* with James Patterson. He's worked as a book publisher, a reporter, a political communications director, and a commissioner for the city of New York. Hart lives in Jersey City.

VISIT ROB HART ONLINE

robwhart.com
robwhart.substack.com
@RobWHart1